ALL THAT OUTER SPACE ALLOWS

THE FOURTH BOOK OF THE APOLLO QUARTET

Ian Sales

Whippleshield Books
www.whippleshieldbooks.com
UK

Published by Whippleshield Books
www.whippleshieldbooks.com

ISBN 978-0-9931417-3-7 (limited)
ISBN 978-0-9931417-2-0 (paper)
ISBN 978-0-9931417-4-4 (ebook)

Edited by Jim Steel
Cover by Kay Sales (kaysales.wordpress.com)

Chapter 1
"We choose to go to the Moon"

Ginny is at the table on the patio, in slacks and her favourite plaid shirt, tapping away on her Hermes Baby typewriter, a glass of iced tea to one side, a stack of typescript to the other. Something, a sixth sense, she's developed it during her seven years as an Air Force wife, a *presentiment*, of what she can't say, causes her to glance over at the gate to the yard. And there's Bob, Lieutenant Colonel Robert Lincoln Hollenbeck, cap in hand, his movie-star profile noble with concern. Ginny immediately looks over to her right, across to the Air Force Base and the dry lake. Her hand goes to her mouth. Oh my God my God my God. There's a line of dark smoke chalked up the endless sky. My God my God my God. She pushes back her chair and lurches to her feet.

Is it...? she asks.

Have you seen Judy? Bob replies. She's not at home.

Ginny's heart takes wing. *It's not Walden.*

No, she says and she's not thinking straight as she knows Judy is out. She's not at home?

She has to ask: It's Scott?

He ejected in time, Bob explains, but he'll be laid up for a time.

The smoke?

His F-104 hit the ground pretty hard.

Ginny knows the F-104, the one that looks like a silver missile. With its stubby wings, its sharp-pointed nose and the great burning orifice of its jet-pipe, it could be a starship— no, a *star fighter*... In fact, that's not a bad idea. She pushes her sunglasses up onto her crown, picks up a pencil and scribbles a note on a piece of paper.

I think Judy has gone into Lancaster, she tells Bob. She'll be back soon.

I guess I better wait for her, Bob replies. She'll want to go see Scott in the hospital.

Is it bad?

Bob shrugs. Busted leg, he says.

I got some more iced tea in the refrigerator.

He shrugs again and settles his cap back on his head. I guess, he says. He seems to realize he's being unmannerly, and adds, Yes, that would be real fine, Ginny.

Ginny leaves her writing—now is not the time to fill her mind's eye with other worlds and other times. She'll tidy everything away later, once Bob has gone, and before Walden gets home. Walden puts up with it but he doesn't like it, and he especially doesn't like to be reminded of it— his wife, the "space cadette", it was funny, kind of endearing even, back when they were courting at SDSU and afterward, when he was in the Air Force and before she graduated, which she always insisted on doing. Since their marriage, Walden has used her writing far too many times as a weapon, a club with which to browbeat her into submission when they argue, when he wants his way and their stubbornness is equally matched. He's a liberal guy in many respects and she loves that about him, and perhaps if he had not been Air Force he'd be something wild and crazy; but he's also a man and he runs roughshod over her wishes and desires every moment of every day. She knows only too well which battles she can fight to the bitter end and which are better served by beating a tactical retreat.

But sometimes, too many times maybe, Walden gets his way, and her stories are where she puts the victories she feels she should have won. They're a form of therapy for her, a *catharsis*, a way of vicariously living out a life the real

10

world can't give her, though she wants it so much, was brought up to demand it, remembering with pain and sadness her mother's bitterness as she was marched back into the kitchen when the Second World War ended, "Rosie the Riveter go back home" tattooed on her heart, written in the lines of her face.

Ginny fetches the jug of iced tea and a pair of fresh glasses, and she and Bob settle down in the lounge, on sofas across from one another, the coffee table between them. Sprawled on its top are half a dozen magazines, the cover of the uppermost depicting a beautiful woman in a bubble helmet exiting a spaceship on an alien world, the name "Alice Eleanor Jones" prominent as the issue's novella is hers—but then she's a big-name author and has been for the past ten years. Ginny only wishes she were as good as Jones (and she's jealous of Jones's success in the slicks). Bob takes his glass, balances it on one knee, his cap now hung on the other knee. Ginny lifts her sunglasses from her crown, bends forward to put them on the coffee table, and uses the movement as an excuse to scoot the magazines together into a pile and then place the pile on the carpet. There's a thin dusting of sand on the table-top and a series of smeared rectangles where the magazines sat—she never moves anything here in the desert, fine sand gathers on every surface—so she gives a swipe with the flat of her hand before sitting back.

For a minute or so, they smile uncomfortably at one another. Ginny likes Bob, he's a swell guy, but they both know this moment is awkward; and she's wondering what possessed her to invite him inside to wait for Judy. He would have been happy sitting in his car, it's not like he can do small talk with a woman, even a "free spirit" like Ginny—that's how Ginny likes to think the guys on the base think of her. (She knows it's probably not true and Walden will tell her nothing; and she tries so much to fit in, even with the other wives but sometimes it's hard and she says something and everyone turns to look at her like she just sprouted a second head.)

This is nice tea, says Bob. Not too sweet.

It keeps me going during the day, Ginny says.

You said Judy went into Lancaster?

Bob takes another sip of his tea, and then glances at his wristwatch.

Ginny looks at her own watch. I'm pretty sure it was about three hours ago, she says. I guess she'll be back any time soon.

Bob rises to his feet. I ought to go wait outside, he says, so I don't miss her.

You'll hear her drive up from here, Ginny tells him.

The room is as silent as the desert, Ginny won't have distractions like the radio playing when she's writing. Her typewritten words drop into her stories like supersonic jet fighters stooping from the sky.

She thinks, was I being forward? Was that forward? I don't want him to read too much into that, maybe I'm being too relaxed. It's only Bob, but... She sits up straight, prim and proper, despite the slacks and shirt, despite the strappy slingback sandals and the chipped polish all too visible on her toenails, and says, But if you think that's best...

Bob nods. I think so, he says.

His face is a mask, but Ginny thinks maybe she detects some relief. And she wonders if spending the morning in the head of her story's heroine is making her see things in that handsome countenance which don't exist, her imagination spilling over into the real world and laying a deceptive gloss over it. It's okay when she's with Walden, she knows him so well, she can read him like, well, like *a book*. And when there's company over, she's usually had all day to prepare for it, to rehearse for the role she must play, dashing from room to room getting them clean and tidy, getting the food ready, getting everything *just right* like she's supposed to...

Bob puts his cap on his head and carefully straightens it. It was nice tea, he says, Thank you, Ginny.

So she rises to her feet, and says, You're coming on Sunday, aren't you? To the barbecue?

Sure, he replies, Alison and I are looking forward to it. He gives a curt nod. You'll tell Wal I was here, he says (and it's clear from his tone it's not a question).

Of course, Ginny tells him.

She sees him to the door, the front door this time, not the patio doors, and she watches as he crosses the road and climbs into his blue sedan. There's a cough and a dyspeptic rumble as the engine starts, but the car remains in place, motor idling, occupant gazing fixedly forward.

Ginny closes the door slowly and returns to the lounge. She tidies away the iced tea, rinsing the glasses, drying them and putting them in a cupboard, returning the jug to the refrigerator. It's getting close to five o'clock and Walden will be home just after six, so she heads out onto the patio to pack up her typewriter and manuscript. She sees the note she scribbled earlier and gazes down at it; and then thinks, Oh my, you silly. F-104. She knows about them, Walden has flown over a hundred hours in F-104s. It's the Lockheed F-104 *Starfighter*. She knows that, why would she write something as silly as "like a star fighter". It was Bob, his appearance threw her.

Ginny gathers up her typescript into a buff folder, and carries it and the typewriter inside. After she has put away her writing things, and the magazines from the lounge, she makes herself ready for Walden. She brushes her hair, puts on lipstick and powder, checks her appearance will pass inspection, and goes to make dinner. It's all part of the job of being an Air Force wife, presenting a normal home-life so her husband can briefly forget how close he comes to "buying the farm" each day. It's a small price to pay, she loves Walden, her love remains undiminished from the day they wed—although that doesn't mean they haven't argued, they haven't spent days refusing to talk to each other.

Ginny's mother brought her up to be independent, to have expectations, ambitions and, okay, marrying an Air Force pilot wasn't the smartest move she could have made in that regard—

Unlike many of her friends, Ginny didn't go to university to catch herself a husband, she stayed and matriculated, married Walden a month after she received her Lit degree. She never used her BA, of course, she joined her husband in the United States Air Force. But she has her stories, she has her imagination, and because Walden allows her that she's willing to play the dutiful Air Force wife for him.

At six thirty, she hears a car pulling up, and then the tigerish roar it makes as it slides into the carport and the engine-noise bounces off the walls. She smiles, her flyboy is home.

He strides into the kitchen minutes later, where she's stirring gravy, puts his arms about her waist, sticks his nose into her hair, breathes in deeply and then plants a kiss on the top of her head.

You hear about Scott? he says.

Bob was here, looking for Judy, she replies.

Damn bad luck. He's going to be grounded for months with that leg.

And that's all Walden says on the matter.

Ginny exits the house carrying a tray on which sits a platter of raw steaks. The guys are standing about the barbecue—Scott in a chair to one side, busted leg held out stiffly before him in a cast. Walden is making some point emphatically with jabs of a pair of meat tongs. She stops a moment and watches them, watches *him*, her husband, wreathed in a cloak of grey smoke, her flyboy, in his white T-shirt and tan chinos, aviator sunglasses, that wholesome white-toothed smile. And she thinks, so strange that his parents should name him after a book subtitled "Life in the Woods"...

They didn't, of course; I did, I named him Walden for Henry David Thoreau's 1854 polemic. There is a scene in Douglas Sirk's 1955 movie *All That Heaven Allows*—the title of this novel is not a coincidence; the movie is a favourite, and, in broad stroke, both *All That Heaven Allows* and *All That Outer Space Allows* tell similar stories: an unconventional woman who attempts to break free of conventional life... There is a scene in the movie in which Ron has invited Cary back to his place for a party. While he and his best friend, Mick, fetch wine from the cellar, Cary is at a loose end and idly picks up a copy of Thoreau's *Walden* lying on a nearby table. She opens the book at random and reads out a line: "If a man does not keep pace with his companions, perhaps it is because he hears a different drummer. Let him step to the music which he hears, however measured or far away." Not only is *Walden* Ron's favourite book, she is told, but he also *lives* it—

Walden Jefferson Eckhardt, however, is indifferent to Thoreau's book, not sharing his parents' admiration of it or its message, for all that he is a test pilot; and they see themselves as a breed apart, at the top of the pyramid, men of independence and daring and achievement. Walden stands there with his fellow test pilots—and Ginny knows them all—and though they're tall and stocky, blond-haired and brunet, craggy-featured and smooth-faced, they all look the same. Cut from the same cloth, stamped from the same mould.

She starts forward, her heels tock-tock-tock on the patio, because for this gathering she's playing the dutiful Air Force wife and has dressed accordingly. She approaches the men at the barbecue bearing bloody meat for them to char and broil, and they turn carnivorous grins on her, teeth bright through the smoke, eyes invisible behind aviator shades.

Hey, Ginny, let me take that, says Al, reaching out with both hands for the tray, the neck of a beer bottle clutched between two fingers.

She hands him the steaks, then turns to Walden. Chicken next? she asks.

He has interrupted his anecdote because it's not for her ears. Sure, hon, he says off-handedly.

Galaxy

FEBRUARY, 1968

VOL. 26, NO. 3

MAGAZINE

CONTENTS

She's tempted to ask him what he was talking about, but she's uncomfortable under the mirrored eyeless gazes of the guys, so she gives a faint smile and tock-tock-tocks away.

The women are sitting about the table at which Ginny likes to write, nursing drinks, their faces powdered and lipsticked, some wearing sunglasses, a couple with fresh hairdos. And it occurs to Ginny there are more stories at that table than there are when she has her typewriter upon it—and they are *real* stories, not the science fiction she writes, which are set on worlds constructed from, and inhabited by, figments of the imagination; nor are they the stories which appear in *Redbook* or *McCall's* or *Good Housekeeping*, what Betty Friedan calls stories of "happy housewife heroines"—and it's those very stories which drove Ginny, and no doubt women like her, to science fiction and its invented worlds. Ginny dislikes words such as "prosaic" and "quotidian" because she believes what she writes employs a dimension beyond that, she believes her stories use science fiction to comment on the prosaic and quotidian *without* partaking of it.

But right now the prosaic and quotidian are signalled by a sky like a glass dish hot from the oven and the phatic chatter of four women in bright dresses, the most colour this yard of sparse grass, and its trio of threadbare cottonwoods, has seen for weeks.

Pam looks up as Ginny approaches, leans forward and slides a martini slowly across the table-top. This one's for you, she tells Ginny.

I still have the chicken to bring out, Ginny replies.

Later, Pam says with a smile. Drink first.

Alison and Connie add their voices, so Ginny takes the free chair at the table and it's a relief to stop for a moment. She lifts the drink and toasts the other women.

These barbecues are a regular occurrence, though they each take it in turn to play host. Here in the Mojave Desert, the days are bright and blue-skied, endless dust and heat, and so they lead summer lives throughout the year. Ginny sips her martini and lets the chatter of Judy, Alison, Connie and Pam, and in the background the boasting of the men, wash over her. She has maybe fifteen minutes before the steaks are ready and Walden starts demanding the chicken; because when he wants something he expects to get it, she's here to cater to him after all. Perhaps in private she can make her own demands, set her own limits, but he brooks no dissent on occasions such as this. She takes another sip of her martini and tells herself her "feminine mystique" is for her husband's eyes and ears only—

Ginny's attention is snagged by the rasp of a lighter, and she looks up to see Judy put the flame to a cigarette in her mouth. So Ginny leans forward and asks how she is coping with her invalided husband. In response, Judy sucks in theatrically, eyebrows raised and lips pursed, and then expels smoke in a long plume over the table. The others laugh. It is all too easy to sympathise, they are Air Force wives. Ginny abruptly remembers days in Germany, when Walden flew F-86D Sabre jets for the 514th Fighter-Interceptor Squadron at Ramstein AFB. For all her open-mindedness, her hankering for new horizons, Ginny found Germany a difficult place in which to live, the contrast between life on the base and life outside, life in the US and life in Europe, too stark, too marked for comfort. She was prolific during those two years, her writing helped her cope.

Walden calls out: Hey, hon, chicken!

No rest for the wicked, says Alison.

Ginny gives an exaggerated sigh, drains the last of her martini and then plucks the olive out of the glass. She pops it into her mouth before rising to her feet.

Later, everyone has repaired to the lounge and the radio is playing quietly in the background. Ginny is sitting on the floor at Walden's feet when he throws a newspaper down onto the coffee table and says to the other guys, Have you seen this?

Bob leans forward and picks up the newspaper, that day's *Los Angeles Times*.

What am I looking at? Bob asks.

NASA wants more astronauts, Walden tells him.

Bob looks down at the front page and reads out: "NASA is looking for men. You must be a United States citizen, not over 36 years old, less than 6 feet tall, with a college degree in Math or Science and with at least 1,000 hours flying time. If you meet all the requirements, then please apply."

Seriously? asks Bob. You thinking of putting your name in?

Yeah, replies Walden. They've put, what, a dozen guys up so far? And the Soviets have launched about ten. They're top of the pyramid now, Bob.

You been keeping track? asks Al (but his grin is a little too knowing).

Ginny is as surprised as the guys, she didn't know Walden was interested in space. Walden has asked about the X-15 program, she knows that; but he has not been assigned to it.

She hopes her husband applies to NASA, and she hopes he is successful. She likes the idea of being married to an astronaut, certainly what she knows of space exploration she finds fascinating and she'd welcome knowing what it's *really* like. Ginny reads and writes science fiction, stories about spaceships and alien worlds, but they're made up, invented. The Mercury program, the Gemini space capsule—they're real, men have used them to orbit the Earth. They're *actual* in a way Ginny's stories can never be.

The other wives at Edwards, and their husbands, they don't know about Ginny's writing. She hides away the magazines when she has visitors—female visitors, of course; the men simply don't see them, much as they don't see anything they consider of interest only to women—and she uses her maiden name as a byline, because she started sending letters to the magazines as a teenager and became known under that name. Ginny keeps her science fiction life separate and secret from her life as an Air Force wife, it's easier that way. But for all she knows there may well be other subscribers to *Galaxy* and *If* and *Worlds of Tomorrow* at Edwards Air Force Base.

Of course, life here is all about the menfolk, supporting them, providing a stable home life to succour them when they're not risking their lives. Perhaps that's why NASA insists on test pilots—or, at the very least, jet fighter pilots. Because their wives are trained to provide the stability the astronauts need in order to risk their lives publicly in such an untried endeavour...

If so, then the joke is on NASA: test pilot marriages fracture before test pilot nerves.

Chapter 2
T-Minus

Walden says nothing about the physical at Brooks AFB or, months later, the interviews at the Rice Hotel in Houston; but for a week after his last trip to Texas he swaggers more than usual. Ginny knows this unshakeable confidence is as much a coping mechanism as will be, should he fail, his subsequent realisation he doesn't really want it anyway. But she hopes he succeeds, she wishes she could go into space herself. But she knows that, at this time, it's an occupation reserved for men—no, more than that: reserved for men of Walden's particular stripe, jet fighter pilots and test pilots. She calls him "my spaceman" one night, it just slips out—she is reading the latest issue of *If*, there's a good novella in it by Miriam Allen deFord, and Ginny's head is full of spaceships and spaceship captains; but Walden turns suddenly cold and gives her his thousand-yard stare. He starts to explain the competition is fierce, he won't know how he's done until he hears from NASA... but he breaks off, scrambles out of bed and stalks from the room.

Ginny puts the magazine on the bedside table, but her hand is shaking. She sits silently, her hands in her lap, and waits. He does not return. Fifteen minutes later and he's still not back, so she rearranges her pillows, makes herself comfortable beneath the sheets, and reaches out and turns off the bedside lamp. She has no idea what time it is when he eventually slides into bed beside her, waking her, and whispers, Sorry, hon. She rolls over, closes her eyes and tries to re-enter some alternate world of sleep where marriages are blissful, life itself is blissful, and she is as famous as Catherine Moore or Leigh Brackett.

They wake at 0430, the shrill ring of the alarm dragging them both from sleep. While Walden goes for a shower, she wraps herself in a housecoat and heads for the kitchen. There is breakfast to prepare—coffee to roast, bread to toast, eggs to fry, bacon, pancakes and hash browns. She does this every day, sees off her man with a full stomach and a steady heart. Here he is now, crisp and freshly-laundered in his tan uniform, hungry for the day ahead. He takes his seat, she pours him juice and coffee, slides his plate before him, and then sits across the table and watches him eat as she sips from a cup of coffee. She should be getting up before him, making herself ready, dressed and made up, to greet him when he awakes—but countless past arguments have won her the right to make his breakfast and see him off to work without having to do so. The housecoat is enough.

They kiss goodbye at the door, and he strides off to the Chevrolet Impala Coupe in the carport. Though she wants to go back to bed, there is too much to do, there is always too much to do.

After clearing up the breakfast things, she makes herself another coffee and settles down to catch up with her magazines, she is a couple of issues behind with *Fantastic*, and this issue, the last of 1965, features a novella by Zenna Henderson and stories by Doris Pitkin Buck, Kate Wilhelm and Josephine Saxton.

Later, she will get dressed—and she will dress for comfort, not for appearance's sake—and she will get out the typewriter and she will work on her latest story. She made the decision years before to incorporate elements of her own life—and, suitably disguised, Walden's—into her science fiction, so she feels no need to visit libraries or book stores for research. She has a stack of issues of *Fantastic Universe*, *If*, *Amazing Stories*, *Galaxy*, *World of Tomorrow* in a closet—they are all the research material she needs. *Galaxy*, after all, runs a science column by astronomer Cecilia Payne-Gaposchkin; *Amazing Stories* has featured science columns by June Lurie and Faye Beslow since the 1940s. Walden, of course, has a library of aeronautics and engineering texts in the bedroom he uses as a den, and

---

"The only women in the group beside myself were Virginia Kidd and Donald Wollheim's wife Elsie, who wrote a little and was nominally called a Futurian."

p44, *Better to Have Loved*, Judith Merril

"Gernsback claims he had as many female readers as male, but far fewer women became actively involved with fandom than men. Despite their numbers, the main route to fandom—having your letters published—was blocked to them, perhaps, as Gernsback implies, because they were less interested in engaging with the science of science fiction than men."

p25, *The Battle of the Sexes in Science Fiction*, Justine Larbalestier

"Not only was the female viewpoint unappreciated in most of the '20s, '30s and '40s, but also women were generally relegated to the position of "things", window dressing, or forced to assume attitudes in the corner, out of the way."

p281, 'Hitch Your Dragon to a Star: Romance and Glamour in Science Fiction', Anne McCaffrey (*Science Fiction Today and Tomorrow*, Reginald Bretnor, ed.)

"What sort of person writes science fiction? He—it is "she" once in about fifty times—very seldom depends wholly on the writing of science fiction for his living."

p51, *New Maps of Hell*, Kingsley Amis

"A few women, such as C. L. Moore and Leigh Brackett, were working in the field earlier; Katherine MacLean entered the fray in 1949 in *Astounding*."

p258, *Trillion Year Spree*, Brian W Aldiss

"But at the same time [science fiction] has always reflected and continues to reflect a particular type of authority, that of men over women."

p87, *In the Chinks of the World Machine*, Sarah Lefanu

Ginny has on occasion paged through them—not that Walden knows: his den is for him alone and she allows him the illusion of its sanctity; naturally, it never occurs to him to wonder how the room remains clean.

Ginny is feeling lazy today. She likes to think she has an excellent work ethic when it comes to her writing, but some days she finds it hard to muster the enthusiasm to bang on the keys of her typewriter. Especially when she has just read something she thinks she can never approach in quality—and that, she sadly realises, is true of the Saxton story in the magazine she is holding. Josephine Saxton is a new writer, from England, and this is her debut in print. Ginny only wishes her first published story, just four years ago in *Fantastic*, had been as good.

The blow to her confidence decides her: she will leave her current work in progress until tomorrow; today she will catch up on her correspondence, she owes letters to Ursula, Judith and Doris, and she really ought to fire off a missive to Cele at *Fantastic* with her thoughts on the issue she has just read.

After she has showered and dressed in slacks and shirt, she finds herself outside on the patio, gazing east across the roofs of Wherry Housing toward the Air Force Base and Rogers Dry Lake, and beyond it the high desert stretching to the horizon, where the Calico Mountains dance in the pastel haze of distance. As she watches, a jet fighter powers up from one of the runways and though it is more than a mile and a half from her, she can tell from its delta wing it is a F-102 or F-106. Its throaty roar crowds the lapis lazuli sky, there's a quick flash of mirror-bright aluminum as the aircraft banks, and then it seems to fade from view as it flies away from her. She wonders if it's Walden in the cockpit, she has no idea what he does from day to day once he enters the base; officially, he's a research test pilot in the Fighter Test Group, but she doesn't know what he researches, which fighters he test pilots. Not the North American X-15, she knows that much, an aircraft which intrigues her because it is also a spaceship—it has flown more than fifty miles above the Earth, right at the edge of space, at over 4,000 miles per hour. And it even *looks* like a spaceship, like a rocket, as much at home in vacuum as it is in atmosphere. She would like to know more about the X-15 but it's a sensitive subject in the house. Walden has tried to get on the program but has been refused, and he wears the refusal badly. Perhaps that's why he was so keen to apply to become an astronaut.

Ginny is a California girl, a *real* one, born and bred in San Diego in Southern California, not one of those "dolls by a palm tree in the sand" from that song on the radio. She has history in this landscape of deserts and canyons and mesas, though she grew up beside the limitless plain of the Pacific. Here in the Mojave she is hemmed in by mountains, they encircle her world, her flat and arid world, where the small towns are so far apart they might as well belong to their own individual Earths. Standing here, gazing in the direction of Arizona, she finds it easy to believe Edwards is the only human place in the world, a lonely oasis of civilisation—and she knows her husband thinks of it as a technological haven in a world held back from the best science and engineering can offer by the short-sightedness of others. To some degree, she thinks he may be right. But she is also a housewife, and she lives in a world in which bed linen must be changed, clothes laundered, meals cooked and checkbooks balanced. She envies Walden his freedom to ignore all that—because she manages his world.

And now she really must get on with her letter-writing, although the lawn looks like it needs mowing and the end of the yard is beginning to look a little untidy...

On Fridays, Ginny drives into Lancaster to do the weekly shopping; there's a commissary on the base but its stock is better-suited to bachelors. Ginny and Walden only have the one car, of course, the Impala, so she accompanies him onto the base and then drives the car back home. He won't let her drive him to work, he has to be behind the wheel, though she's a perfectly good driver, not that he will ever admit it.

Since Ginny has to make Walden's breakfast and be ready to leave when he does, she wakes earlier than him in order to shower, dress and make up. She slides out of bed, leaving a sleeping Walden, who breathes as though he were engaged in an endless sequence of underwater dives, and pads across the bedroom to the bathroom. She showers, she washes her hair, she checks her legs and underarms to see if they need shaving; she towels herself dry and wraps it about her torso, and makes turban of a second towel for her hair. She heads for the second bedroom—which is her room in much the same way the third bedroom is Walden's den. He thinks her room contains only clothes and cosmetics and shoes (her wardrobe is not as big as Walden believes it is)—but her closet is actually filled with back-issues of science fiction magazines, nor does he notice the bookcase holding science fiction paperbacks and a few hardcovers. There is no desk, however, only a dressing-table with a triptych of mirrors on its top. Ginny sits before this and minutely inspects her face...

By the time Walden appears in the kitchen, washed and uniformed, Ginny is dressed in a lemon yellow short-sleeved A-line summer dress, bought in San Diego during her last visit and not made from a pattern as the other wives would have done (although Ginny is not, perversely, jealous of their facility with sewing machine, needle and thread), face powdered, eyelashes mascaraed and mouth lipsticked, and her purse waiting on the table in the hall. She dishes out Walden's breakfast and watches him eat it while she sips a coffee. She does not need to glance at her watch to know if they are on schedule—Walden is military, his life is ruled by schedule; he entered the kitchen at the same time he does every weekday, he takes as long to eat his eggs, bacon, hash browns and pancakes as he always does, he pushes back his chair, drains the last of his coffee, and says, Time to go, hon—right on schedule.

And because it is Friday, she replies, yes, dear. And she

rises to her feet, puts his plate and cup, and her own cup, in the sink to be washed later, follows him into the hallway, where she slides on her sunglasses, picks up her purse, and tock-tock-tocks out of the house and into the carport, and waits deferentially while Walden locks up behind her. Once he has slid behind the steering-wheel, she joins him in the car and sits there waiting compliantly as he gives the ignition key a quick, confident twist.

It's the first day of April, the temperature is in the low seventies and the sun beats down on the blacktop, causing it to shimmer and flex ahead of the car as Ginny drives the thirty miles to Lancaster, her foot heavy on the throttle. Tucked away somewhere in her purse is a shopping list of groceries, but as well as the Alpha Beta Market she also needs to visit Sears to buy herself some more clothes. She and Walden argued a couple of evenings ago—he came home angry after some incident on the flight line, he wouldn't say what. She had spent the day writing, he asked in a cold hard voice why she has to dress like a hippy, which only demonstrated to her he has no idea what a hippy looks like, but the remark sparked a fight... And now she must, as she has reluctantly promised, dress more often like the other wives, in skirts and dresses. She is already thinking how she might use the incident in a story, perhaps something about how wives disguise their true nature by presenting themselves according to their menfolk's wishes and expectations, using all the tricks and tools at their disposal: makeup, foundation garments, skirts and heels and the like; maybe, she thinks, the wives could be alien creatures, forced into their spousal roles in order to survive...

There are certainly days when Ginny feels like an alien creature—or rather, days when she feels she has more in common temperamentally with some invented alien being than she does her husband of seven years. Walden is not a complicated man, but there are times when she cannot understand what is going through his head. She knows some of it is a result of a peculiar kind of blindness—he pretends not to see her science fiction, and has done for so long now he probably *can't* actually see it. His mind filters out anything not of his masculine world. If Ginny leaves out a magazine, a copy of *Redbook*, perhaps, or *Ladies Home Journal*, brought round by one of the other wives, Walden says nothing but behaves as if it exists in a blind spot in his vision. When Ginny leaves pantyhose to dry in the bathroom, he complains of her "mess" but cannot say what the mess is. And should Ginny lose something, a lipstick, an earring, he will happily look for it but he will never find it, she has to do that herself, and she often discovers it in a place where Walden has already searched.

She twists the steering-wheel and directs the Impala into the Alpha Beta Market's parking lot, causing it to wallow queasily as it bounces over the edge of the road. She finds a parking space quickly and slots the car into it. After slipping her nyloned feet from the flats she wears for driving into her high-heeled pumps, she exits the Impala; and, as she leans in to pick up her purse, she hears her name called. Surprised, she turns about and there's a figure across the lot waving at her. It's another woman, another wife, blonde hair, sky blue A-line summer dress, tanned arms. And it's a moment before Ginny recognises Mary, wife of Captain Joe H Engle, whom she doesn't know all that well as Mary's husband is a pilot on the X-15 program and Walden is still sensitive on the topic. But the four of them have spoken on occasion in the Officers Club on the base, so if they're not friends then they're certainly acquaintances.

The two women meet up at the entrance to the supermarket and it's clear Mary has something she wants to talk about, although it's not easy to read her expression due to the large sunglasses she is wearing.

Joe tells me, she says earnestly, Wal is doing the tests to be an astronaut?

He is, Ginny confirms. Joe too?

They walk into the store side by side, through the

sliding doors and into its air-conditioned interior.

You think Wal has a chance? asks Mary.

He thinks so, Ginny says.

When do you think they'll be told?

Ginny pulls a shopping cart from the line and drops her purse into it. I don't know, she says. Soon, I hope. I'm not sure I can put up with Walden like this for much longer.

She smiles to take the sting from her words, but the memory of the fight with Walden still burns.

Oh I know, says Mary. Joe's the same, he's not good with all the waiting, you'd think he'd be used to that being a test pilot, wouldn't you?

Joe already has an astronaut pin, hasn't he? Flying the X-15?

The what? Oh I don't know, I guess.

Mary pushes her shopping cart alongside Ginny's and the two make their way, heels clattering, cart wheels squeaking, along the aisle in formation. As they pick items from the shelves and freezers, they discuss what selection by NASA might mean, both for their husbands and for themselves. It's something Ginny, who has only really thought about the technology of space exploration, the launch vehicles and spacecraft, the science and engineering, has not considered. She has a book she has been reading, hidden in her underwear drawer where Walden will never find it: *Americans into Orbit* by Gene Gurney, "The Story of Project Mercury". One day, she hopes, Walden will be in such a book. The issues raised by Mary are ones that have not occurred to Ginny: not only moving to Houston and finding somewhere to live, but being in the public eye, she's seen the interviews in *Life* magazine, she's seen the astronauts and their wives on television, she knows several of them have been invited to the White House and met the president, and there were ticker tape parades in New York for some of the Mercury Seven. Ginny wonders if she wants that—not that she will have any say in the matter if Walden is selected.

If they ask him, he *will* accept—and nothing she can do will prevent him.

The telephone rings but before Ginny can get to her feet, Walden is up and striding into the hallway. She hears him answer, and then it is a succession of yes sir, of course sir, I would be honoured sir, yes sir, I'll be there sir, *yes sir.* Someone from the base, she decides; and returns to her book. Moments later, Walden marches into the lounge and he is grinning fit to break his jaw.

That, he says, was Deke Slayton.

Ginny recognises the name. He is one of the Mercury Seven, although he never flew since he was diagnosed with a heart murmur. She remembers his headshot from page 89 of *Americans into Orbit.*

From astronaut selection at NASA, Walden adds.

She doesn't need to ask, she can tell from Walden's expression.

I report in four weeks, he tells her.

You're going to be an astronaut, she says; and she doesn't quite believe it. She puts down her book. An *astronaut*, she says again in wonder.

He crosses to her, bends forward, grips her about the upper arms and hauls her to her feet. I am! he crows. I'm going into space!

He wraps her in a tight hug and she can feel the righteousness beating off him like waves of heat. She can also feel where his fingers wrapped her arms and pressed hard enough to bruise.

You might even go to the Moon, she says.

She can't help it, she's grinning too now, she is as excited as he is.

Shit, yeah! The Moon! I'm going to the goddamn Moon!

He whirls her around, and she laughs giddily. Then he pulls her in close again and he says, I wanted this, Ginny, I really wanted it, I wanted it so bad.

You deserve it, Walden, she tells him, you're the best.

She wraps her arms about his neck and pecks him on the cheek—because she's happy for him, *more* than happy for him, his joy is hers too; and because she loves him.

And later, she knows, he will prove his love for her in his own way.

NATIONAL AERONAUTICS AND SPACE ADMINISTRATION

MANNED SPACECRAFT CENTER NASA Houston 1, Texas

HU 3-5111

MSC 66-22
April 4, 1966

HOUSTON, TEXAS Nineteen pilots will join the astronaut team early in May, the National Aeronautics and Space Administration announced today.

They will boost the total number of NASA astronauts to 50.

Average age of the group is 33.3 years. Average number of college years 5.8, and average flight time is 2,714 hours, of which 1,925 hours is jet time. Two of the new astronauts have doctorates. Two are single.

Four civilians are among those selected. Of the remainder, 7 are Air Force officers, 6 are Navy Officers, and 2 are Marine Corps officers.

They include:

Vance D. Brand, 34, an engineering test pilot for Lockheed assigned to the West German F-104G Flight Test Center at Istres, France. Brand, his wife and 4 children live at Martigues, France.

Lt. John S. Bull, USN, 31, a test pilot at the Naval Air Station, Patuxent River, Maryland. Bull, his wife and son live on the base.

Maj. Gerald P. Carr, USMC, 33, Tests Director Section, Marine Corps Air Facility, Santa Ana, California. Carr, his wife and 6 children live in Santa Ana.

Capt. Charles M. Duke, Jr., USAF, 30, instructor at Aerospace Research Pilot School, Edwards Air

Force Base, California. Duke, his wife and one son live in Edwards, Calif.

Capt. Walden J. Eckhardt, USAF, 32, experimental test pilot, Edwards AFB, Calif. Eckhardt and his wife live in Edwards.

Capt. Joe H. Engle, USAF, 33, aerospace research flight test officer assigned as project pilot for X-15, Edwards AFB, Calif. Engle, his wife and two children live in Edwards.

Lt. Cdr. Ronald E. Evans, USN, 32, on sea duty in the Pacific. His wife and two children live in San Diego, Calif.

Maj. Edward G. Givens, Jr., USAF, 36, project officer at the NASA Manned Spacecraft Center for the Astronaut Maneuvering Unit (Gemini experiment D-12). Givens, his wife and two children live in Seabrook (El Lago), Texas.

Fred W. Haise, Jr., 32, NASA project pilot at Flight Research Center, Edwards, Calif. Haise, his wife and 3 children live in Lancaster, Calif.

Dr. Don L. Lind, 35, physicist at NASA Goddard Space flight Center, Greenbelt, Maryland. Lind, his wife and 5 children live in Silver Spring, Md.

Capt. Jack R. Lousma, USMC, 30, operational pilot at Marine Air Station, Cherry Point, North Carolina. Lousma, his wife and one son live in Newport, N.C.

Lt. Thomas K. Mattingly, USN, 30, student in Aerospace Research Pilot School, Edwards AFB, Calif. He is single and lives on base.

Lt. Bruce McCandless, III, USN, 28, working toward a doctorate in electrical engineering at Stanford University. McCandless, his wife and two children live in Mountain View, Calif.

Lt. Cdr. Edgar D. Mitchell, USN, 35, student in Aerospace Research Pilot School, Edwards AFB, Calif. He has a doctor of science degree from Massachusetts Institute of Technology. Mitchell, hs wife and two daughters live in Torrance, Calif.

Maj. William R. Pogue, USAF, 36, instructor in Aerospace Research Pilot School, Edwards AFB, Calif. Pogue, his wife and 3 children live at Edwards.

Capt. Stuart A. Roosa, USAF, 32, experimental

test pilot at Edwards AFB, Calif. Roosa, his wife and 4 children live in Edwards.

John L. Swigert, Jr., 34, engineering test pilot for North American Aviation, Inc. He is single and lives in South Gate, Calif.

Lt. Cdr. Paul J. Weitz, USN, 33, squadron operations officer. Weitz, his wife and two children live on Oak Harbor, Washington.

Capt. Alfred M. Worden, USAF, 34, instructor at Aerospace Research Pilot School, Edwards AFB, Calif. Worden, his wife and two daughters live in Edwards.

Recruiting of the new astronauts began Sept. 10, 1965. A total of 351 submitted applications, of which 159 met basic requirements. Of that number, 100 were military, 59 civilian. For consideration, applicants must have been a United States citizen; no taller than 6 feet; born on or after Dec. 1, 1929; have a bachelor degree in engineering, physical or biological sciences; and have acquired 1000 hours jet pilot time or have graduated from an armed forces test pilot school.

—)—

Chapter 3
Liftoff

A month after the telephone call, Walden rents a car, leaving the Impala with Ginny, and drives to Houston, where he stays in a motel with some of the other guys from Edwards. Of the nineteen astronauts NASA has selected, nine, including Walden, are from Edwards Air Force Base. Ginny jokes in a letter to Joanna that the air of Edwards is so thick with the "Right Stuff", with a miasma of testosterone blown this way and that, it drives the wildlife into reproductive frenzies. She's not entirely joking—she has seen the other wives ballooning with fecundity at, to her, shockingly short intervals. She and Walden have only been here four years, but surely the streets didn't used to ring quite so loudly and so frequently with the insistent laughter of children?

It is something they have fought about. Ginny is not yet ready to be mired in motherhood, made subservient to her so-called biological clock. Nor is she willing to make a young child a hostage to Walden's good fortune. It is her most telling argument, her one true defence—she will not agree to children while the chance exists Walden might be killed.

Walden calls her the evening of his arrival in Houston—she has spent the day catching up on correspondence, there are so many people she wants to tell that her husband is now an astronaut; she feels guilty for boasting about it, but oh she feels so *righteous* in her bragging. She and Walden try to plan their immediate future. He will stay in the motel, and in his free time will look for somewhere more permanent to live. And then Ginny will join him.

Two months later, she packs up the Impala, having made arrangements for the contents of the house on 16th Street to go into storage until sent for, and sets off on the 1,600-mile drive to her husband. She heads south to San Diego and spends the night with her mother and step-father in the house his successful landscape gardening firm has given them (though Ginny's mother is the business brains). Ginny welcomes spending time in a properly organised world, where everything has its place because that's the *right* place for it, not because military tradition, or orders from on high, say it is. There is a comforting sense of sanctuary, which Ginny feels especially keenly given her and Walden's abrupt change in circumstances and location—not just the 1,600-mile move, but the glamour, the science, the complex engineering and, above all, the danger of Walden's new career.

It *is* dangerous, darling, isn't it? asks mother, conveniently ignoring that test piloting is dangerous, that flying fighter jets in Germany is dangerous, that Ginny's father was a naval aviator who did not survive the war—and whose haloed absence during her formative years no doubt led Ginny to romanticise pilots and so now she's been married to one since graduating from SDSU.

No one has died, Ginny tells her. They've had all those Mercury flights and Gemini flights, and everyone splashed down safely.

Ginny cannot know she will be proven wrong before a year has passed. On 27 January 1967, no more than six months away, there is a fire in the Apollo 1 command module during a plugs-out test at Launch Complex 34. The crew of three, Gus Grissom, Roger Chaffee and Ed White, all perish. The Apollo program will be delayed for over eighteen months as the spacecraft is redesigned to rectify the defects which led to the tragedy. Ginny will spend that day weeping, like many of the other astronauts' wives, not only because she knows the three widows, although not closely, and she knows the men, although barely at all, but

35

because she has rudely learnt, as has every astronaut wife, that her husband flirts with jeopardy to a level she has not previously contemplated or wanted to believe.

It is perhaps unfair to characterise Ginny as happily ignorant of the perils of spaceflight, and those specifically of the Apollo space program. She writes about space travel, after all; but in her stories it is all so easy, spaceships flying up into the heavens and zipping about the galaxy as if it were no more onerous than a cross-country flight in a plane or an ocean crossing aboard a liner. But that's not entirely true—she has learned to live with the daily prospect of a uniformed stranger with a grave expression appearing on her doorstep, much as Lieutenant Colonel Hollenbeck did in the first paragraph of this novel. That incident not only illustrated the danger of Walden's chosen profession, but showed also that Ginny's immunity to it is no more than skin-deep, a thin veneer of confidence no thicker than a layer of Revlon's "Touch & Glow".

And yet... The romance attached to NASA's astronauts, to the organisation's roster of successful space flights, makes Ginny believe her man is indeed safer now. Perhaps she only *wants* to believe it, as she gazes across the split-level lounge at her mother sprawled elegantly on a sofa, gimlet in one hand, cigarette in the other; and Ginny looks down at the gimlet in her own hand, and all she can think of is a softly-moaning desert beneath a sky like a dome of pure blue ceramic, and her imminent drive across three states through a landscape no different, to reach her husband, who may be going to the most desolate desert of them all on the surface of the Moon.

Ginny leaves early the next day, setting out on a California July morning that promises freshness but will no doubt soon blur to muggy haze, turning her back on the ocean, though she has not lived within sight of it for many years, and aiming the Impala at Tucson, Arizona. The US Highway

80 runs west out of San Diego, through the chaparral and canyons of the Cucamaya Mountains, across the green checkerboard fields of the Coachella Valley south of the Salton Sea, and down into the Sonoran Desert.

I could perhaps pass quickly over the long drive east, much as Apollo 16 astronaut Charlie Duke does in his autobiography *Moonwalker*: "Man, I'm an astronaut. I've got it made! I thought to myself as we rolled into Houston." Or, as Willie G Moseley writes in his biography of Apollo 14 astronaut Stuart Roosa, *Smoke Jumper, Moon Pilot*: "the family traveled from California to Houston in a long station wagon". Or even James Irwin, whose place in the space program Walden Jefferson Eckhardt has taken in this story, who wrote in his book, *To Rule the Night*: "I drove down to Houston in my little Kharmann Ghia and reported in at NASA May 10."

Journeys, however, are important in people's lives, although they are probably accorded more importance than they strictly deserve in fiction. They're not simply, in narrative terms, a relocation but also a metaphor for change—and for Ginny and Walden, great change has indeed entered their lives. This lonesome drive across Arizona and Texas is a threshold moment for Ginny. She is alone in the car, often alone on the road, in the desert, with nothing but herself and perhaps intermittent radio stations for company. She has been briefly enfolded in the maternal bosom, but now she is once again independent, her own woman—albeit linked to her husband of almost eight years by a strong thread of love and respect, and still identified in official correspondence as Mrs Walden J Eckhardt, as if she possesses no name of her own, no history prior to her marriage. Perhaps the landscape she drives through reflects her changing moods, perhaps it triggers trains of thought which speed alongside the Impala as it follows the endless asphalt, accompanied only by the hum of the car's tyres, the throb of its engine and the whistle of the wind. She wonders if the surface of Mars resembles this near-lifeless land, she considers writing a story about the Red Planet. She remembers a serialised novel in *Analog* last year which was set on a desert world, where tribes from the

```
Dearest VeeGee,

How wonderful, wunderbar, mervielleux! Your man
is going to the stars--well, not so far, of
course, only we get to make that journey, and in
our imaginations too, a vessel so much better
furnished than the shiny metal spaceships of
NASA. I am so very jealous of how close you will
be to it all, right there at the side of the
launchpad--that is what they call it, isn't it?
I cannot deny it exerts an ineluctable, albeit
masculine, fascination. That our lovely
spaceships of the mind should be translated into
these towering edifices of steel and flame. It
seems horrifyingly apt they were developed from
missiles. But: still there is that pull, that
inescapable tug on our sense of wonder which
comes from seeing our metaphorical voyages from
star to star turned into something so real and
palpable, etc. The years ahead will be an
exciting time for you--but I hope you don't find
them too onerous you stop writing, that would be
a loss unbearable. There are few enough of us as
it is. Look after your astronaut, my dearest
VeeGee, but look after yourself too--that wild
imagination, that incisive intellect of yours,
they both need regular exercise. Keep up the
good work, sister!

                                        YouKay
```

deep desert fought Imperial occupiers who had seized their planet to control a unique substance required for interstellar travel. The author's name was Frances, but they all knew it was a man—editor Kay Tarrant, conscious of her magazine's readership, felt a female pen-name more appropriate.

The Impala is not fitted with air-conditioning and once

out of the mountains the interior of the car quickly heats up. Even with the windows down, the air is close and seems to possess a hot and smothering weight. Ginny has anticipated this and is wearing a pair of white cotton shorts, but when the backs of her thighs begin to stick to the seat she realises she has chosen badly. She feels quite invisible in this vast empty landscape, a brightly-coloured mote adrift on a sea of sand grains... But she proves sadly all too visible when she stops for gas at a station on the outskirts of Tucson. The shorts, her bare legs, attract male attention, not just eyes she can feel creeping all over her, but comments and whistles too. She's not in California now, she has spent too long in military society, it has slipped her mind the impact a lone woman, especially an under-dressed one, might have among male strangers. She pays for her gasoline quickly, eager to return to the solitude of the road.

The route from San Diego to Houston is very different in 2015 to how it existed in 1966. A single Interstate, I-10, now stretches from Santa Monica, California, to Jacksonville, Florida, crossing the state of Texas at its widest point. Much of I-10 was built during the 1970s and so predates Ginny's migration—and sometimes not everything required for research can be found online. This is one of the perils of writing a story set in the past and in another nation, "a different country" in both senses of the phrase.

Ginny spends the night in a motel in El Paso, and the following morning she dresses more comfortably, and modestly, in a mid length checked cotton skirt. She takes to the road early, driving south out of El Paso, scrubby desert to either side and the road running runway-straight through it, and off to her right a line of dark green marking the fertile valley of the Rio Grande, and beyond it the tumbled purple blocks of the Sierra Madre louring on the horizon. She finds the scenery bleak and oppressive and elects to push on, thirteen straight hours behind the wheel;

and though San Antonio promises a welcome haven when she reaches the city in the evening, she presses on and arrives in League City just after nine at night.

Walden seemed unconcerned at the prospect of her "solo flight", and his directions to the apartment he has rented in League City are perfunctory—she has to forgive him, he has other things on his mind—but she finds the Cardinal Apartments easily enough, turning off the Gulf Freeway onto Main Street, and there it is, on the other side of US 75 in one of the new subdivisions, at the top of Texas Avenue, two or so miles from the junction.

She slips her bare feet into her sandals, clambers from the Impala and stretches. Pulling her sunglasses from her crown, she throws them onto the car's bench seat, and then turns about and regards her surroundings. The Cardinal Apartments, looking more like a motel than an apartment complex, with a balcony giving access to second floor apartments. But the area is certainly greener than she has been used to, greener than the Mojave around Edwards with its bent and twisted Joshua trees, greener than the scrubby garden of their house on 16th Street, greener than the desert she has spent the last day driving through. She can see the black clouds of trees against the glowing night sky across the street, and hear the conspiratorial whisper of their leaves in the faint breeze. From somewhere over the trees, the hum of traffic faintly intrudes. The temperature is about eighty, a little warmer than Edwards. She turns back to the apartment building, and is hit by a flood of tiredness. In a single moment, she feels all those hours of driving, and her lack of motion gives her a sharp and momentary sense of vertigo, a brief spin of nauseating dizziness.

It was a long drive, and an echo of those hours behind the steering-wheel seems to hang in the dark and muggy air, but she thinks she might like it here, this sprawling verdant city, with its subdivisions of low houses and wide featureless lawns, so very different to the desolate sandy expanses of Edwards; and though she can taste the bite of pollution in the air, her heart lifts.

Which is more than Mary Irwin, wife of James Irwin—and the "role" Ginny is playing in this novel—felt in her autobiography *The Moon is Not Enough*: "But as we entered Houston after three days of cramped travel in our camper without airconditioning, and as I saw the murky pall of smog hanging over the city, and felt the muggy, suffocating heat, a little part of me withered inside."

From her purse, Ginny pulls out the scrap of paper on which she has scribbled the address given her by Walden. At one end of the apartment building is a staircase leading up to the second floor, and from the apartment number on the paper, her new home must be up there. She locks the car and climbs the stairs, and is soon standing before the door of the right apartment. She knocks.

Moments later, the door swings open and there is Walden, his face bearing that frown Ginny knows he wears when he has been interrupted at some important task. She smiles wanly at him. His eyes widen, his arms open, he grins and steps forward and pulls her into a hug. She is so tired she almost falls against him.

She is home.

—))—

Chapter 4
Pitch and Roll Maneuver

Those first two months in the apartment, Ginny spends her days at the typewriter. New places always have this effect on her—until she feels settled she exorcises her discomfort with the written word. It was the same in Germany, though she never grew used to life in that country; and she did this too when Walden was transferred to Edwards and she found herself living in Wherry Housing. She has explored this new home of hers: the apartment building, the city and its meagre shopping clustered at the junction of US 75 and Main Street, the scattered subdivisions either side of the Gulf Freeway. There is nothing to see here, and even less to do. Walden disappears into the Manned Spacecraft Center every day, leaving her to her own devices, and though there are several astronaut families in the area and in the Cardinal Apartments—including Dotty and Charlie from Edwards—the other wives have their kids to keep them occupied. She sees the women in the yard and on the street and at the stores, and she stays on friendly terms with them, even offers to provide transport on occasion for those who lack it, since Walden has left her the Impala. (All of the astronauts will be paid ten thousand dollars per year by *Life* magazine for exclusive rights to their stories. Walden has used some of the money to buy himself a car he feels better suited to his new career.)

Ginny sits at the table in their one-bedroom apartment and travels to the Moon and beyond in her imagination. She writes three stories in short order. But a deputation from the Astronaut Wives Club, a social club founded that summer by Marge Slayton and Louise Shepard, Ginny has already missed two of the monthly meetings, it's four of the New Nine wives calling round to see her. Faye, Marilyn, Pat and Barbara, there to welcome Ginny into the fold, to her new life in "Togethersville"; but she is writing and when they see her in slacks and rough shirt, and the typewriter

---

Hugo Awards 1966

Awarded at Tricon, Cleveland, 1 September 1966 – 5 September 1966

NOVEL
- **Winner (tie):** "…And Call Me Conrad" (AKA **This Immortal**), Roger Zelazny (*F&SF* Oct, Nov 1965; Ace)
- **Winner (tie): Dune**, Frank Herbert (Chilton)
- **The Moon Is a Harsh Mistress**, Robert A. Heinlein (*If* Dec 1965, Jan, Feb, Mar, Apr 1966; Putnam)
- **Skylark DuQuesne**, E. E. Smith (*If* Jun, Jul, Aug, Sep, Oct 1965)
- **The Squares of the City**, John Brunner (Ballantine)

ALL-TIME SERIES
- **Winner:** "Foundation", Isaac Asimov
- "Barsoom", Edgar Rice Burroughs
- "Future History", Robert A. Heinlein
- "Lensman", E. E. Smith
- **The Lord of the Rings**, J. R. R. Tolkien

SHORT FICTION
- **Winner:** "Repent, Harlequin! Said the Ticktockman", Harlan Ellison (*Galaxy* Dec 1965)
- "Day of the Great Shout", Philip José Farmer (*Worlds of Tomorrow* Jan 1965)
- "The Doors of His Face, the Lamps of His Mouth", Roger Zelazny (*F&SF* Mar 1965)
- "Marque and Reprisal", Poul Anderson (*F&SF* Feb 1965)
- "Stardock", Fritz Leiber (*Fantastic* Sep 1965)

---

on the table, they purse their lips and she gets the lecture. It's all very friendly, they sit in the apartment's tiny lounge, drinking Ginny's coffee, some of them smoking. Barbara talks about the need for the right breakfast, a "hot, nutritious breakfast" in NASA's own words, but Ginny already knows this, she's a test pilot's wife, she had the "5 am breakfast" lecture years before.

This is tougher than being a test pilot's wife, says Marilyn, ten times tougher.

What you do, adds Pat, reflects not only on your husband but on NASA, on the USA.

Ginny is in the public eye now, they tell her; she must at all times be proud, thrilled and happy. And well-groomed, always well-groomed.

But there are rewards. Once your husband has flown in space, says Barbara, you get to go places and meet people. NASA likes to have us there at parties and functions, like an astronaut's accessory.

This generates knowing laughter from the other three New Nine wives.

Gemini 11 is due to launch next week, which means to date seventeen astronauts have been into space, some of them even twice, including the husbands of both Faye and Barbara.

Faye leans forward and puts her coffee cup on the carpet by her feet. There should be no problems at home, she says, looking up at Ginny, nothing that might jeopardise your husband's chance of a flight. You need to stand by your man.

...her words eerily presaging the song, which is released a couple of weeks later, although Ginny does not hear it until months have passed. Tammy Wynette may be a native of Mississippi, but in 1966 the song's sentiments are universal.

The women leave after an hour. Despite the 85°F heat, Ginny opens the windows to dispel the smell of cigarette smoke and commingled perfumes worn by the wives. She looks back across at the dining table and the Hermes Baby sitting on it, and wonders that they never thought to ask her what she had been typing. Perhaps the clothes she's wearing shocked them so much it slipped their minds. She is amused at the thought: the slacks and shirt are mannish but she could never be mistaken for a man. Nor for some sort of genderless human being, neither man nor woman—and a line of thought, no doubt triggered by the hot humid air pushing its way into the room through the open windows, has her imagining a race of androgynous people who, like many animals, are only sexually active when in heat, and then they can be one sex or the other. It's not a bad idea for a story, she thinks; but she decides not to make a note of it—no way to use it occurs to her and it's not an idea she feels qualified to explore.

The next month, on the first Tuesday, Ginny puts on makeup, more than she usually wears, and a dress bought in Neiman Marcus only the week before, styles her hair, and drives over to the Lakewood Yacht Club for her first AWC meeting. There are forty-eight of them now, drinking tea and coffee and nibbling on cakes and cookies in the ballroom. Ginny spots Pam, but she also recognises Mary, and Dotty too, of course, and she sees Louise, another Mary, Joan and Wanita, who were also at Edwards. Ginny doesn't know most of the other wives, so Pam and Dotty help out with the names, but it's too many to take in at once, and Ginny is feeling a little uncomfortable, something of an outsider at this gathering, as she can see how closely knit the various groups are, how confident and assured and *polished* are the wives of the Original Seven and the New Nine. It occurs to her that her standing in this group is a consequence of her husband's achievements. Right now, he's just one of the new guys, spending his time in a classroom training to fly the new spacecraft. He may never go to the Moon, he may never even make it into space. The real pioneers are the ones who have flown; and their wives are golden in the reflected glory. There's Louise, the Boston Brahmin, in white gloves; and Rene, as Ginny has heard, does indeed look very glamorous—and Pam tells Ginny in a whispered aside that Rene has been writing a newspaper column, 'A Woman, Still', for the past year. It's a connection, Ginny thinks, we're both writers—except Ginny writes science fiction and she's pretty sure Rene is not going to consider that equivalent to a newspaper column; there's no way the lurid covers and contents of *Galaxy* or *If* or *Fantastic* can compete with the prestige of the *Houston Chronicle*.

Not that it matters, anyway. Even at Edwards, Ginny didn't feel much like an Air Force wife, a test pilot wife, though she took care to make all the right noises. And this astronaut thing is too new—she's read books on Mercury and Gemini, she's seen the photographs of the missions in *Life* magazine, the space walk last year; but a connection between *that* and this room full of smartly-dressed women seems too fanciful to willingly suspend disbelief.

She feels a fraud, perhaps because she dressed up especially for the AWC, and she's awkwardly aware Walden shares a deeply competitive camaraderie with these women's husbands which defines all their lives, men and women alike; but she also knows she's considered little more than some sort of domestic technician by NASA, just another government employee, engineering the home—what's that phrase in *The Feminine Mystique*? "women whose lives were confined, by necessity, to cooking, cleaning, bearing children". By *necessity*. There to keep the astronaut home running smoothly, her own wants and needs, her "mystique" not a factor in the equation, not mentioned in any scientific papers or training manuals, not part of the plan to put a man on the surface of the Moon. And return him safely to the Earth.

Much as Ginny would like to avoid the AWC and its monthly meetings, she knows she has no choice.

She is an astronaut wife now.

Ginny has been thinking about a story, prompted by something she read in a book, *Invisible Horizons* by Vincent Gaddis, a paperback, with a waterspout prominent on its cover, the title above it in bright green letters. Where did she find this book? I don't know—perhaps she bought it in the Edwards AFB commissary, although I don't know if they sell books; perhaps it was the same place she found a copy of *Americans into Orbit*, a book store on a weekend trip to Los Angeles, or on a visit to her mother and step-father in San Diego. While I own *Americans into Orbit*, the 1962 Random House hardback edition, I know very little about *Invisible Horizons* as I've not been able to find a copy, I can state only that it was originally published in 1965 by Chilton Books, the same publisher who took a chance on Frank Herbert's *Dune* in that year. Ginny's edition of *Invisible Horizons* is the Ace paperback also published in 1965. One chapter in the book caught her interest, an alleged experiment in 1943 to turn a US Navy destroyer invisible—which will later enter occult science mythology on the publication of Charles Berlitz's book *The Philadelphia Experiment* in 1979, Berlitz being best-known at that time for his 1974 book on the Bermuda Triangle. None of this, of course, is known to Ginny, who has simply happened upon something in a book which she thinks might make a good premise for a science fiction story.

And so she wonders what it might be like to be aboard a ship as it fades from sight while beside her the contractor tries to explain how the house will look once built; but she's gazing out across an empty plot of land staked out by wooden posts where one day walls and windows and doors and roof will materialise, as if brought into being by the passage of time, and the invisible warship in her mind's eye morphs into a spaceship. She turns to the contractor, flashes him a smile as if she has heard, understood and agrees with every word he has spoken. As he leads her across the plot toward the dirt road, where his Dodge D Series pickup truck sits behind her Impala, and he swings out an arm and says something about a kitchen, it occurs to her that her story would be more interesting if she told it as *her* story, as a wife's story. Ginny has stood in a kitchen, wondering if her husband will come home that day, knowing that every morning as he leaves for work he might be killed or injured. She has tried to make a sanctuary for him of their home for that very reason—and for all her independence and need for "mystique", she loves Walden too much to jeopardise the fragile balance between his work and his home, his sanity and his safety, or even the good standing in which he is held by his current employers.

I guess that's everything, Mrs Eckhardt? says the contractor.

He pulls open the driver's door to his truck, and now Ginny can't see the name emblazoned on it because she's just come up blank, her head full of story, of an image of herself standing at the stove, and superimposed over it, a ghostly overlay, another woman in some future fashion—perhaps a dress made of small white plastic discs which shimmer and clack when she moves, Ginny thinks she saw something like it in *Vogue*, which of course she does not read herself, it must have been in the beauty parlour, or perhaps when visiting Pam or Mary or Dotty or Joan—

And so she gives another bright smile, puts a hand up to adjust her sunglasses and says, yes, yes, of course, thank you so much.

The contractor holds out a hand to shake, and she looks down at it, briefly disconcerted, and then takes it, his rough workman's hand enfolding her own with the painted nails she has yet to get used to—the time it takes to keep them shaped and polished!—she feels like she should be a completely different person, not the Ginny whose body she has been inhabiting these thirty years but another person, weak and frail, with her soft red-nailed hands, powder and paint, pantyhose and heels.

It's all part of the astronaut package. The past few months of parties, the press gatherings, even the television appearance, at all of which her husband has been dutifully accessorized with her, and she has remained polite and noncommittal—but enthusiastic about space, NASA and Walden—they have been exciting times, intoxicating even, after their years of exile in the desert. And the money she has spent so she can look the part! Walden has his new car, but when he demands to know where all the money is going he is blind to the fact she's wearing a new outfit.

Ginny tells herself all this is fair payment so the man she loves can do what he so dearly wishes to do: go into space, perhaps one day walk on the Moon; but in her increasingly more frequent self-critical moments she knows she's only fooling herself, making the charade palatable. For the possibility of Walden on the lunar surface, she will keep herself "pretty", she will dress like the other astronaut wives, she will be thrilled, happy and proud.

And smile until her jaws ache from the hypocrisy of it all.

Months later, Ginny will regret her moment of inattention when she learns she apparently agreed to something she doesn't recall. Walden is furious and believes the contractor unilaterally decided it for himself, but Ginny, if only to deflect his rage, admits it may have been her fault, she had misunderstood or misheard the man. In time, they'll come to appreciate the contractor's choice, but for now it sours their pride in their new house, which Ginny feels is only fair since the pride seems to be mostly Walden's—as if he built the house himself, as if he personally oversaw its construction. She hasn't the heart to tell him she apparently used the "wrong" contractor, not the one the other astronauts used, and some of the wives have been unpleasant to her about it. *That* sours her sense of achievement.

It doesn't help that days after breaking ground on the plot in El Lago Walden and Ginny had bought, Gus, Roger and Ed die in a fire in the Apollo 1 command module. Ginny, who knows Betty, Martha and Pat only passingly as fellow members of the AWC, like all of the wives feels the deaths keenly because it seems a tragedy she believed the best of science and engineering worked to guard them against; but now all of their husbands are hostages to the same fickle fortune—and the fact none of them has been able to take out life insurance becomes suddenly and horrifyingly and heart-breakingly *relevant* and *real*. It's not simply the all too imaginable prospect of a future without their husbands which stabs so deeply, but a stripping from them of their own purpose.

This is not strictly true, of course. At this point in the story, it may be 1967 but women are not chattels, although the Equal Pay Act only became law four years before—a chief campaigner for which was, coincidentally, one of the Mercury 13, Janey Hart. It would be foolish to pretend the United States has actual gender equality. Women had not been given the vote until 1920; and whatever freedoms they may have enjoyed during the Second World War were rudely taken from them when the GIs returned home—as illustrated by the appearance of Ginny's mother in this story in the previous chapter.

Though it may seem the astronaut wives do little but keep house, mother their children and worry about their husbands, many also have other interests, or even part-time jobs—Rene, as mentioned earlier, is a newspaper columnist, and later becomes a radio host and television presenter; some wives are substitute teachers; others are heavily involved in the activities of their local church or community theatre. But some are indeed only wives and mothers, as Lily Koppel writes in her book, *The Astronaut Wives Club*, about Pat White: "She had dedicated everything to him. She had cooked gourmet meals. She had handled all his correspondence... 'She just worked at being Ed's wife,' said one of the wives, 'and she was wonderful at it, and that was all...'"

Ginny has years of practice at dreaming up possible futures, but she weeps because Apollo 1 suggests a future she begs providence to keep purely fictional. Walden has always been, and remains still, the brightest star in her map of the galaxy; and she cannot bear the thought of life without him. So she spends days privately weeping for a loss she has not experienced and may never experience;

and then she wipes her eyes and fixes her mascara and joins the rest of Togethersville in succouring the new widows.

Later, once the funerals are over and life has returned to what passed previously for normal, although perhaps it is a little more tightly wound, Ginny, who is often inclined to ascribe attributes, either luck or inevitability, to things which do not possess or deserve them, feels the tragedy may blight their new house, might perhaps apply itself to Walden's career. But she is not a foolish or suggestible woman, if anything she likes to think she sees the world as operating along rational lines, according to fixed physical rules and laws, not all of which have yet to be discovered, a consequence she believes of her choice in literature, of the magazines to which she subscribes, avidly reads and contributes—

Which, sadly, she has not been doing as frequently as she had. Keeping up appearances, showing the other wives she is a reliable member of the community, attending the meetings and parties, dropping by others' houses, having people drop by hers...

She's rarely alone, even though Walden is not often at home, he's either at the Cape all week; or when he's in Houston, he's at the Manned Spacecraft Center and when he gets home in the evening his head is too full of orbital mechanics, spacecraft systems and the manuals he has been studying to care about Ginny's day. It's a level of disengagement an order of magnitude greater than at Edwards, Walden eats his late dinners in silence, and then spreads all his books and manuals across the kitchen table, or relaxes in front of the Zenith colour television, Space Command 600 remote control loosely held in one hand, to watch the football or a current affairs show.

Perhaps this is just as well. Ginny has been finding it increasingly hard to cope with being an astronaut wife. It has been weeks since she last wore slacks, and her favourite plaid shirt sits folded and unworn in a drawer. The Hermes Baby has only come out of its case a half-dozen or so times since her first meeting of the AWC, and then only to write letters—and she still owes replies to many of her friends.

Since moving to Houston, Ginny has not left the city, she has not been to the Manned Spacecraft Center, she has not seen a rocket or anything related to the space program. Walden has brought lots of paperwork home, and she's sneaked looks through some of it when he's not about. But surreptitiously checking out Walden's training materials—she loves the Apollo spacecraft, their lines, their detail, their immense complexity, all those dials and switches, she wants to know all there is to know, much as she would about a spaceship which appeals to her on the cover of a magazine—but it's only diagrams and dry text and what she really wants is to climb inside a LM or sit inside a CSM, she'd like to stand beside a Saturn V and actually *experience* its immensity. But she's reluctant to display too much interest, Walden has professed on more than one occasion that he much prefers his "new" wife, and although she feels like a robot replica of Virginia Grace Eckhardt more and more of the time, in a town of robot wives which were designed, of course, by and for men—and now she thinks about it, that's not a bad idea for a story—she nonetheless maintains the façade, the pretence: because everything on the home front must be "copacetic" if her husband is to have a chance at the Moon.

Her "space cadette" days are behind her, or so Walden believes—but he remains, as ever, mostly oblivious.

---

was not the only writer of the first half of the twentieth century explicitly writing about the female experience, and using science fiction to do so.

The place of Virginia Grace Parker, who was published under the gender neutral name V. G. Parker, in the canon of feminist science fiction has been under debate for more than two decades. She was not a prolific writer, producing only eleven stories in as many years. Her stories were interesting for their general atmosphere of isolation, initially filtered through the experiences of a wife or mother. In this, Parker's fiction followed the form of "housewife heroine" stories, as defined by Betty Friedan in her landmark work, *The Feminine Mystique*. Classic examples in science fiction include Judith Merril's "Only A Mother" and Alice Eleanor's Jones's "Created He Them", both of which are very much products of the Cold War and which explicitly document a housewife's response to a situation resulting from a nuclear war. Parker, curiously, never based stories on this trope, and it is tempting to speculate the fact she was married to a serving US Air Force officer gave her a different perception on nuclear weapons' capabilities and likelihood of use.

Parker's stories fall into three rough periods, each corresponding to changes in circumstances linked to her husband's career. The early ones were written while Parker lived in Germany. They were often told from the point of view of an alien, and displayed a somewhat pessimistic view of humanity. But once Parker's husband had been stationed back in the USA, the stories turned more optimistic and more domestic, culminating in "The Spaceships Men Don't See". This last story is especially interesting, and not simply because its title eerily presages James Tiptree, Jr.'s 1973 story, "The Women Men Don't See".

"The Spaceships Men Don't See" was published in *Galaxy* in 1968. The story describes a secret military project to develop a spaceship which is invisible to the enemy. The main character of the story is the wife of an engineer who is working on the project. It is not going well, and as the engineer returns home each evening, his wife can tell that the day has once again been a failure. This distancing from the central *novum* of the story—the technology required to render the ship invisible is neither explained nor provided with pseudo-scientific scaffolding—is common to much "housewife heroine" science fiction.

The story was rejected by a number of magazines before Frederik Pohl took it for *Galaxy*. However, he asked for several changes before he would purchase it. In the original version, it was only the presence of women which was required to trigger the invisibility field. Pohl thought the story might have more impact if the presence of women *and women only* were needed for the invisibility to work, and asked Parker to rewrite the final third with that in mind. She did more than he had requested, however. Not only did she change the ending to imply that men would no longer be capable of waging war, in a bold move she also removed all the male characters' names and referred to them only by their relationship to the female characters. Particularly interesting is the character Betty—possibly named for famous aerobatics pilot Betty Skelton—whom the men treat like one of their own, because she is a test pilot. And Betty in turn treats the wives in the same fashion as the men—except during that one moment of solidarity in the final paragraphs of the story.

There is a strange note of bitterness to Parker's description of the relationship her protagonist, Suzanne, has with her husband. It is implied they have sex, and that it is not especially frequent in their marriage. Perhaps Parker intended this to be an ironic reflection of the husband's failure with his secret project. But she also hints his moment of amorousness in the story is either a consequence of Suzanne's appearance—she has dressed up for the wives' social—or of the husband spending time in the social club bar with Betty.

"The Spaceships Men Don't See" proved unpopular with many of the magazine's readers, and one particularly scathing letter writer declared he was not interested in "womanly gossip and high heels", and that readers of *Galaxy*, had they been interested in "women's affairs" would be reading "a woman's magazine". Perhaps embarrassed at this vitriol, the editors did not reply to the letter and even neglected to mention that V. G. Parker was not male, as the correspondent had assumed, but female. However, it was likely Parker's gender was known to most readers—she made no effort to hide it, unlike James Tiptree, Jr.—although there are no contemporary records of any science fiction fans, authors or editors actually meeting her in person. During the fifties and sixties, women were not common at conventions—and those that did attend were typically married to a fellow attendee, or had a professional relationship with the genre. Given that Parker's husband was in the military, it's reasonable to assume attendance at a convention would have been frowned upon, even if her husband had permitted it.

Despite the controversy following the publication of "The Spaceships Men Don't See", the story quickly vanished into obscurity. Feminist commentators have criticized it on a number of grounds. The female characters, although foregrounded in the narrative (it is *their* story, not their husbands'), have almost no agency. Even the story's resolution is a consequence of their gender, rather than any action any of them have taken. The wives are also characterized by their clothing—in fact, the only colors mentioned, other than grey, refer to the garments worn by the women. It is likely Parker's use of color was intended to be ironic, rather than pandering to nineteen-sixties conceptions of where women's interests lay.

Parker's final period was prompted by her husband's selection as an astronaut by NASA. He eventually flew to the moon aboard Apollo 15. It is possible the response to "The Spaceships Men Don't See" precipitated a new direction in Parker's writing, and she chose to use her proximity to the space program to add a more marked technical sensibility to her science fictions, something not present in works by other women writers of the period—and this was a decade in which 250 women began writing for genre magazines. This level of technical detail reached an almost obsessive degree in her last published work, the novella "Hard Vacuum", about a group of astronauts marooned at a lunar base. The science fiction written by women at this time, however, was considered to be "soft", and despite her command of her subject, Parker had great difficulty breaking into the all-male "hard" science fiction club. She sold only three stories, in addition to her novella, and those sank without trace.

Parker stopped writing science fiction after the appearance of "Hard Vacuum". Two space-related non-fiction works, and a co-writing credit on her husband's autobiography, appeared during the following decade, before Parker finally faded from sight.

Chapter 5
Max-Q

Ginny looks down at the sheet of paper she has just fed into the typewriter and she thinks about a title for this story she can feel taking shape in her mind. She thinks about the word "invisible" and its synonyms, but then she decides she needs to make invisibility an *act*, not a property—the ships are not hidden from sight, people simply *do not see them*.

She types,

<u>THE SPACESHIPS MEN DON'T SEE</u>

Yes, she likes that.
And on the next line,

by Virginia G. Parker

Her name, her byline. The letters which identify this story as something created by herself, even though she herself is a creation, a fictional construct. Virginia Grace Parker, who I named for three actresses of the 1950s—Virginia Leith, Grace Kelly and Suzy Parker—and whose life bears a passing resemblance, in parts, to those women I researched in the writing of this novel—especially Mary Irwin, wife of Apollo 15 astronaut James B Irwin, but also science fiction authors Judith Merril and Alice B Sheldon. However, Ginny Eckhardt née Parker is more than the sum of her inspirations, more than an invented history patchworked from the lives of others; and she leans forward and narrows her gaze as the first sentence of her story comes to her, and she types:

Once a month, the wives of the test
pilots and engineers ~~met up~~ gathered at
the social club for coffee and
conversation.

Walden is away at the Cape, she has not seen him since the weekend; and the small apartment is quiet. Ginny has her imagination, and a network of friends spread across the country, and she uses them to fill the empty hours. And, of course, there is the AWC, members of which are all too prone to drop by or telephone, to chat, to have a drink, coffee or something stronger, to just be company, whether she wants it or not. But somehow she has managed to free up today, although she has an appointment tomorrow at the beauty parlour so she will look her best when Walden flies home from the Cape on Saturday. For now, her thoughts are centred on the world of her heroine with the spaceship research pilot husband, a deliberate echoing of her own situation. She thinks about an invisible Navy destroyer in 1943, about pantyhose hanging from a line across the bathtub and lost earrings and women's magazines sitting on coffee tables. She considers her role as an astronaut wife and the pressure to conform exerted by NASA and the other wives; and her mind is drawn to the Apollo spacecraft, the command module and lunar module, so exhaustively detailed in the manuals Walden studies so assiduously. She thinks about the fiction she has read in her magazines over the past six months, stories by Linda Marlowe, Kit Reed, Anne McCaffrey, Monica Sterba, Susan Trott, Betsy Curtis, Joan Patricia Basch...

And the words flow from her, this is one of the easiest stories she has ever written, perhaps because it had such a long gestation, perhaps because so much of herself is in it— and the narrative does not require those mental gymnastics she must usually perform if, say, her story were set among the crew of a spaceship on some endless voyage landing on an alien world for the first time. She is writing about the Astronaut Wives Club and the Apollo astronauts, although she knows no one reading this story—should she manage to sell it—will ever see the connection.

She works right through lunch, forgetting the salad she made the day before which is sitting in the refrigerator, neglecting the cooling cup of coffee beside the typewriter, and even forgetting that she is improperly dressed for the task, not wearing her slacks and favourite shirt but a short-sleeved shift dress in pink, orange, gold and green paisley. It is mid-afternoon by the time she types the words,

The End

—pulls the sheet of paper from the platten and sets it face-down on the pile beside the typewriter. She turns over the manuscript and carefully lines up each page until the corners are square.

Sitting back, she feels an ache lay itself across her shoulders like a yoke. A deep sense of satisfaction fills her, a heartfelt gratitude that the past year has not taken from her the ability to write science fiction. She knows the story will need going over with a sharp eye, but she is happy with this first draft.

Her coffee is too cold to drink, so she slips her shoes onto her stockinged feet, and heads to the kitchen to brew herself a celebratory cup.

And if mention of Ginny's feet in nylons seems an odd detail to include, there's a line in *The Astronaut Wives Club*, "Even when she wore her 'at home' slacks and went barefoot, she always put on her makeup", about Martha Chaffee, wife of Roger, a homecoming queen at Purdue and described by Koppel as "drop-dead gorgeous". It's for good reason Koppel repeatedly likens Martha to Twiggy—those bare feet! only hippies go around in bare feet! Martha was plainly a bit of a free spirit, a tad "individual".

Unlike Martha, Ginny has given up her "at home"

clothes, she is trying hard not to be "individual". Because she and Walden are childless, the other wives feel no compunction to call ahead when dropping by. Ginny has had the lecture once, and she knows Walden's feelings on the matter; let them see her doing as she's told, she still has "Virginia G. Parker" and not one of them knows about her.

The following morning, she goes over the story once again, but it needs only minor changes and takes her no more than forty minutes to type out a final draft incorporating them. She writes a quick cover letter to Evelyn at *Galaxy*, puts it and the typescript into a large envelope and, on her way to the beauty parlour, drops it into a mailbox.

That Saturday night, Ginny and Walden are watching television, he has a beer, she's skimming through an issue of *Good Housekeeping* but the contents are boring her, when the telephone rings. Ginny puts down her magazine gratefully, goes to answer the phone and it's Evelyn from *Galaxy*.

This story, Evelyn says, I like it, I like it a lot, but I think you need to fix the ending.

Ginny is proud of 'The Spaceships Men Don't See', she thinks it's the best story she's ever written, and she doesn't like hearing that it's not perfect. But she also knows that Evelyn knows her stuff, she's an excellent editor and has been doing this for over a decade. Besides, if changes are needed to sell the story, Ginny is happy to make changes.

What do you mean? she asks.

Evelyn elaborates, You tell the story from the wife's perspective, and you drop plenty of hints she's the solution, but you don't actually explain the consequences of what happens. You need a twist, Ginny; readers need to know there's a reason it's her story and not his.

"The reason for how the story ends..." Ginny realises not only is Evelyn right about the story but her words describe

Ginny's own life here in Texas equally well. The Apollo flight schedule has been postponed while the Apollo 1 fire is investigated and the Block II command modules brought up to scratch. Though it has been six months, a pall continues to hang over Houston, adding a bite of melancholy to the ever-present pollution. Impatience too—the astronauts are not so foolish to rush into anything which may jeopardise their lives, but they're keen to start flying again. In Ginny's case, the lack of flights has meant the astronaut wives have been getting on with their own lives: avoiding the press, church work, community theatre, substitute teaching, charitable activities and so on. Ginny has none of these, she has only Walden and her science fiction—and the house being built, arguing with the contractor, only for Walden to apologise to him on his next visit home, angering her at his disloyalty and prompting yet another fight...

So Suzanne, says Ginny, referring to the heroine of her story, you think Suzanne needs to figure out why things happen the way they do?

No, that won't work, you've made it clear she's no scientist, Evelyn points out. But there's an obvious consequence to what happens in your story and you need to spell that out. Perhaps you should put Suzanne's husband closer to the mystery, make him an engineer or something?

But, Ginny thinks, Walden is a pilot, not an engineer; he's not involved in the design of the Apollo spacecraft, although he does need to understand how their every part functions. While his inability to see so many things which are clear to Ginny provided the inspiration for the story, perhaps she should do as Evelyn suggests and give her protagonist's husband more of an investment in the success of the invisibility project. Yes, she likes that idea, and as she works through the ramifications of that change, the perfect ending suddenly comes to her, one that turns everything on its head—

I think I have it, she tells Evelyn.

She describes her idea, without going into too much detail as she knows the narrative will shake itself out as she puts the words down on the page, and right now the new direction of 'The Spaceships Men Don't See' is little more than an unmarked path leading to "The End".

Evelyn laughs. She likes the idea, there's an irony there she says her readers will recognise. Do that, she tells Ginny, write it like that and send it me. As soon as you can. I want that story for my magazine.

Ginny puts the telephone down. She's happy she's sold a story, but it is bittersweet as she thought the original version good enough. No, now she thinks about it, she realises Evelyn is right—this new version is much, much better.

She returns to the lounge.

Who was that, hon? asks Walden, not looking away from the television.

Just one of the other wives, Ginny replies.

THE SPACESHIPS MEN DON'T SEE

V. G. PARKER

He couldn't see the solution to his problem—but his wife could!

Once a month, the wives of the engineers and administrators gathered at the social club for coffee and conversation. Being confined for months on end to the spaceyard, due to its remoteness, was no fun. They all went a little stir-crazy after a time. The men had their work... but what did the women have?

So the wives put on their best dresses, congregated in a back-room at the social club, and gossiped. They oohed and ahhed over the latest fashions in their electronic magazines, and they pretended their coffees didn't contain something a little extra.

Suzanne was looking forward to the social, just as she did every month—although perhaps more this time. Her husband, a project engineer, had been especially distant during the past few weeks. Each evening, he came home from work, and she took his portable computer and his coat from him, and put them away. He said nothing, not even a thank you, just went into his study and closed the door. And the next day, the level of liquid in the whiskey bottle he kept in there had dropped a couple of inches. His work wasn't going well. Suzanne didn't need to be an engineer to see that.

The first person Suzanne spotted when she entered the room at the social club was Kristin, whose husband was one of the spaceyard's senior administrators. Suzanne was immediately taken with Kristin's dress in rich purple, complimented her on it, and was praised in turn for her own pink, orange, gold and green paisley dress. Kristin had also dyed her hair a silvery blonde. "It's very sophisticated, don't you think, darling," she told Suzanne, patting her abundant curls with one hand. "My man loves it, he says I look like a tri-dee star or something."

Kristin could afford to boast—not only was she beautiful and wore the loveliest clothes, but her husband wielded a lot of power in the spaceyard. It wasn't that Suzanne felt grateful for Kristin's friendship—she *liked* Kristin, and knew the sentiment was returned—but sometimes she couldn't help feeling a little resentful at Kristin so frequently calling attention to her many advantages.

They moved further into the room, greeting the other wives in their dresses of yellow and blue and red and other colors, and made their way to the table where the coffee and cakes were laid out. While Kristin poured them both drinks, Suzanne complained about her husband's recent surliness.

"He hardly speaks to me when he gets home," she said. "One evening, he complained his steak knife wasn't sharp enough and went to get another from the kitchen. He couldn't find them

and flew into a terrible rage. It was awful. And do you know where the steak knives were? In the first drawer he looked in!"

"Men are always like that," Kristin said knowingly. "We've been in our apartment for five years now, and my man still can't find the electronic dishwasher."

"And if I ask him to fetch something of mine," Suzanne continued, "like a pair of shoes or some jewellery, he can never find them—even if I give him exact directions!"

Kristin nodded in agreement. She leaned in and lowered her voice conspiratorially. "They're under stress, darling. It's this project they're working on," she murmured. "Project Philadelphia it's called."

"What's that?" Suzanne knew nothing about her husband's work. She was aware the spaceyard built ships for the navy, for the war against the Regulans; but that was all she knew.

"I shouldn't tell you this," said Kristin, "but..." She placed her purse on the table, slipped a small bottle of whiskey from it and added a dash of liquor to her coffee. "They're trying to make spaceships invisible. They've got a destroyer ship down in a special dock, and they've built all this weird equipment into it. It's supposed to make the spaceship completely invisible. He says the theory all adds up, but no matter what they do everyone can still see the spaceship."

Kristin sipped her coffee, frowned, and added a few more drops of whiskey. "There's even been a couple of 'accidents', something about a crewman getting phased into the decking or something." She shuddered. "It all sounded very gruesome, darling."

By this time, several of the other women had gathered round them, and soon they all had whiskey in their coffees and had been told all Kristin knew about Project Philadelphia. Some of the other wives added details to Kristin's account, learned from their own husbands.

Of course, all this knowledge meant nothing. Suzanne couldn't help her husband with his work, but at least she now understood the reason for his bad mood each evening. She even felt a little sympathetic. It must be difficult to work so hard on a project, only for it to repeatedly fail.

After the social had ended, Suzanne waited in the room for her husband, but he didn't appear. He had told her he would come and fetch her. After ten minutes, she went looking for him. She checked her porta-phone but he hadn't called her, and although she briefly considered ringing him she didn't want to seem impatient or demanding. So she left the room and headed for the club foyer. As

she passed the archway leading into the main bar, she happened to glance through it.

And there he was, standing at the bar with the spaceyard's only female test pilot, Betty, who was still dressed in her flightsuit.

Betty turned toward Suzanne as she approached her husband and gave her a flat, hard stare. He, however, hadn't noticed her and didn't turn around until she stood beside him.

"Oh hi, honey," he said. "You know Betty."

He put his whiskey on the bar, turned and pecked his wife perfunctorily on the cheek.

"I thought you were coming to fetch me?" she asked, trying hard not to sound petulant.

"I couldn't find you," he replied. "I swear I looked in every damn room but I couldn't find any of you." He shrugged. "I figured you'd walk past the bar on the way out so I came in here to wait."

He couldn't have looked very hard. He needed only to find a room full of women in their best outfits, and there she would be.

"I must be going," Betty said abruptly. She drained her tumbler, put it on the bar, nodded at Suzanne's husband and strode from the room.

"I guess you're ready to go too," he said.

Suzanne smiled wanly.

Her husband finished off his whiskey and took her by the

elbow.

The spaceyard lights were on night-cycle, and the stars shone brightly through the forcefield dome. Somewhere out there was Earth, too far away to be visible with the naked eye. Even the Sun was an unremarkable point of light in a heaven of stars. Suzanne shivered. She gripped one of her husband's arms and hugged it. During the day, when the lights shone so bright they hid the emptiness of outer space on the other side of the dome, it was easy to forget the spaceyard was sited on a chunk of rock somewhere on the outer edges of the Solar System. Its exact location was, of course, a closely-guarded secret.

Suzanne's husband put an arm about her shoulders and crushed her to him. He was humming some tune under his breath. Perhaps he'd had more than one whiskey in the bar. Or perhaps his good mood was a consequence of Betty's presence. Suzanne wasn't sure she liked Betty, since the test pilot never mixed with the wives and treated them with the same level of detachment as the husbands. If there was any bond there due to their shared gender, it was well hidden.

In bed that night, Suzanne's husband was more loving than usual. He didn't turn his back on her and go to sleep as he usually did. Suzanne tried to persuade herself it was because she'd prettied herself up for the social and her appearance had awoken his slumbering affections. But she suspected she was only fooling herself.

The guard had to ring ahead, and once Suzanne had been cleared, he gave her a security pass to wear. The route from the yard's entrance to the building containing her husband's office was clearly signposted, and she had no difficulty finding her way. The site was very secure—no one could get in unless they were supposed to. In fact, her presence drew several questioning glances from various people, but they said nothing after spotting the security pass pinned to a lapel of her lemon-yellow cardigan style jacket. And they were people she knew, friends of her husband and husbands of her friends. Inside the building, she found herself walking along a corridor lined with windows overlooking the docks, so she stopped to take in the view. Each of the docks, a rectangular pit some six hundred feet long and a hundred feet wide, was identified by large numerals painted onto the concrete before it. The spaceyard was busy: the docks were filled with spaceships in various stages of construction. She spotted a dock off to one, and wondered if that was Project Philadelphia. But the spaceship berthed within it looked no different to any of the others.

Suzanne's husband looked up in surprise when his secretary ushered Suzanne into his office. He frowned on seeing who it was, then came around from his desk and put a concerned hand to her shoulder. "What's up, hon?" he asked. "Is there something wrong?"

"There's nothing wrong," she assured him. "I'm here for the guided tour."

He turned away and swore under his breath. Striding across to his desk, he jabbed a finger down at his intercom. "Nirmala," he snapped. "I'm going to be out of the office for—" He glanced back over his shoulder at Suzanne, who was smiling uncertainly— "For about thirty minutes," he said. "Maybe an hour."

Returning to Suzanne, he added, "I don't know why you want to see the docks. You won't understand anything, and I'm really busy at the moment. I wish you women could have picked a better time."

"Is it because of Project Philadelphia?" she asked.

He glanced at her sharply. "How do you know about that? It's supposed to be top secret."

"Kristin told me."

"She shouldn't know herself. But I guess that's her husband's problem."

They left the office and took an elevator to a higher floor, which was obviously for senior management: the linoleum floor was now carpeted and the walls were covered in discreetly patterned wallpaper. They stopped before an imposing double-door and, after a nod at the secretary sitting behind a desk to one side, the door swung open. This was the office of Kristin's husband, and it was three times the size of a project engineer's, with a deep carpet, a large polished steel desk, some upholstered plastic chairs, and a wall of television screens giving views over the entire spaceyard. Standing before the desk were three men and four women. Suzanne recognised Kristin straightaway, and with her were Eniola, Layla and Aiko. Their husbands were project engineers too, and they were the only other wives who had declared an interest in a tour of the docks. Kristin's husband had agreed to it because, she claimed, he couldn't refuse her anything.

Kristin's husband, who had been sitting behind the desk, rose to his feet and led the small party out of his office, into an elevator, and out of the building onto the large open area fronting the docks. There were fifteen docks arranged in three rows. To the right were workshops and hangars and that single solitary dock, and to the left storage yards and tank farms.

After being led past docks one through five, while their husbands explained the progress of each spaceship and its construction, and then back up past docks ten to six, Suzanne had to admit she was bored.

"Is that Project Washington?" Suzanne asked her husband, pointing at the spaceship in a dock to one side of the other fifteen.

"Philadelphia," he snapped, "it's Project Philadelphia. And yes, it is."

"Can we have a look at that? It sounds really exciting—an invisible spaceship!"

After some discussion, Kristin's husband decided it was permissible for the women to be shown around the Project Philadelphia spaceship. In fact, since there was no work being done on the spaceship at the moment, it was the perfect time for a tour of her interior.

She was far from prepossessing. Her sleek hull was battered and streaked, and the great round engine bells of the spacedrive were blackened and charred. The five women stood at the railing beside the entrance ramp to the spaceship and gazed, puzzled and a little fearful, at its battle-scarred bulk.

"The United Earth Space Ship *Aldridge*," said Kristin's husband.

"She's a Procyon class destroyer. Normal crew is sixteen, but we only use six for this project."

"To make her invisible?" asked Suzanne.

"Yes, to make her invisible. I won't explain how it works." He gave a forced laugh. "You have to let us keep some secrets, you know."

"Let's go aboard," one of the other men said.

Suzanne's husband led the way up the ramp and through the open airlock into the UESS *Aldridge*. Both airlock hatches had been left open, and from the inner one a straight passage led both forward and aft. The party headed toward the bow. The interior of the destroyer was exactly how Suzanne had pictured it: grey metal decking underfoot, grey metal walls to either side, light-fittings enclosed in grey metal guards, grey metal hatches every ten feet. She felt a little silly, walking along that grey military gangway in her burgundy peplum jacket and matching skirt. All five of the women wore brightly-coloured outfits: burgundy and orange and scarlet and lilac and aquamarine. It was as if a flock of tropical birds had invaded the spaceship.

The party came to a steep staircase, a "ladder", and the wives halted in consternation. It looked too steep to climb in high heels, but the women were reluctant to remove their shoes because they might get a run in their nylons. Since they had no choice, the wives ascended the ladder as carefully as they could.

"We should have put them in overalls," complained one of the husbands.

The men all laughed.

At the end of the upper passage, they stepped through a hatch and onto the ship's bridge. It was a cramped space, filled with acceleration couches and consoles, with readouts and dials and buttons and switches on every available surface. Suzanne's husband leaned forward and flicked a set of switches on an instrument panel on the roof. There was loud *thunk*, causing a couple of the women to give muted shrieks, and then a horizontal line of bright light appeared at the front of the bridge. It slowly widened, dispelling the dimness, until a wide forward-looking viewport was revealed.

"Armoured shutter," explained Suzanne's husband.

He took her elbow and directed her further forward between two of the acceleration couches. "The pilot sits here and the astrogator here. Over there is where the sensor tech sits, and behind him is the engineer. The captain sits at the back there, and beside him is the head gunner, the torpedo man and the fireman for the space lance."

Suzanne had to admit this tour was proving less interesting than she had expected. She only hoped it would make her husband feel more comfortable talking to her about his work, so he wouldn't lock himself away in his study every evening. Nonetheless, she smiled and tried to appear engaged but, looking about the bridge, she saw exactly the same expression on the other wives' faces.

Something began to make a noise outside, a strange whoop-whoop unfamiliar to Suzanne.

One of the men swore: "What the hell's going on?"

Kristin's husband pulled a porta-phone out of his pocket and spoke quickly into it. "There's a fire in workshop thirty-two," he informed the other men.

"That's right next to tank farm fourteen!" exclaimed Eniola's husband.

"If that goes, we lose half the stores," Layla's husband pointed out.

The men pushed their way to the bridge hatch.

"What about us?" asked Kristin.

"Stay here," ordered her husband. "Don't touch anything. I'll send someone to come and fetch you."

The men hurried off the bridge.

Kristin shrugged theatrically. "Well, ladies," she said, "so much for that. I guess we ought to make our way back to the main door, or whatever it's called."

"Oops," said Aiko.

Something began to thrum deep in the spaceship. The deck began to vibrate and a smell of ozone filled the bridge.

"Oh my God!" said Kristin. "What have you done, darling?"

"I didn't see the button," Aiko protested. "Look, it's not even supposed to be here, it's like it's just stuck on or something."

They all started bickering. Kristin was blocking the exit from the bridge, and Suzanne wanted to leave the spaceship. She didn't like it in here—even with the window uncovered, there were too many dark corners. Layla complained there was oil on her lilac skirt and she'd never get it clean. Eniola was scared of whatever it was Aiko had switched on—out of fear of what the spaceship might do or what her husband might do Suzanne could not tell. Aiko was adamant it wasn't her fault—whatever it was—and Kristin was determined they stay where their husbands had left them.

Aiko and Kristin snapping at each other started to annoy Suzanne, so she made her way to the front of the bridge, hoping she might see the men returning through the window. She thought about sitting in one the acceleration couches, but it would mean clambering over the armrest and she couldn't do that in her skirt and heels. She could see some figures strolling toward the dock. As they drew closer, she recognised her husband. And with him were the husbands of the other women.

As the men reached the dock, they stumbled to a halt and gazed up at the spaceship. They looked this way and that, some put their hands to their brow to shade their eyes. One of them pointed along the length of the dock at something, and suddenly they were slapping each other on the back, shaking hands and looking very pleased with themselves.

"Kristin?" said Suzanne. "Can you come here a moment?"

"What is it, darling?"

Kristin asked Aiko to be quiet with a raised hand, and wormed her way to the front of the bridge to stand beside Suzanne.

"Look at them," Suzanne told her. "Why are they behaving like that?"

"I've no idea," replied Kristin. "But that humming noise is really starting to get on my nerves."

"Now what are they up to?"

They watched the men run along the side of the dock to the ramp leading up to the hatch. One of them stepped onto the ramp and hesitantly approached the side of the spaceship.

Five minutes later, Suzanne's husband arrived panting on the bridge. "What the hell did you do?" he demanded.

All of the women pretended not to know what he meant.

"One of you did something," he insisted.

"We've got absolutely no idea what you're on about, darling," declared Kristin.

"The invisibility!" he exclaimed. "It works!"

Another figure appeared in the bridge hatch. It was Layla's husband. "Did you turn it off?" he asked.

Suzanne's husband turned to him. "Turn what off?"

"The field. As soon as you entered the ship, it became visible."

"I haven't touched anything."

"I can still hear that hum," Kristin complained.

"What did you do?" demanded Suzanne's husband.

"I don't remember," replied Aiko, either because she truly didn't or because she was afraid to admit she had done anything at all.

Suzanne's husband began to herd the women from the bridge. They trooped along the corridor until they reached the top of the ladder. The two men clambered down it, and the women followed gingerly. Halfway down, the heel of one of Eniola's scarlet pumps stuck in the edge of a tread. Layla was behind her. While the two struggled, the rest followed the men to the airlock and out of the spaceship onto the ramp. Suzanne saw Kristin's husband look up in surprise. He grabbed one of the other men and

pointed at the women. No, *past* them. Suzanne looked behind her. What was the problem? There was the UESS *Aldridge*, looking just as large as life, its grey bulk filling the dock.

Eniola and Layla appeared in the airlock. Eniola was limping, but not because she was injured, and complaining of a run. As the two of them stepped through the hatch and onto the ramp, the men began to talk excitedly amongst themselves.

It took the men less than thirty minutes to determine that the invisibility field only worked when two or more of the women were aboard the spaceship. A single man, however, and UESS *Aldridge* remained stubbornly visible. It wasn't just Suzanne, Kristin, Eniola, Layla or Aiko, either. The men fetched secretaries and nurses, and they too triggered the invisibility. But no man could do it. Aiko eventually confessed to having pressed a button, and it proved to be the main power switch for the invisibility field generator. None of the settings had been changed from the last test, which had of course been unsuccessful, before the wives had boarded.

The men began to talk among themselves.

"I don't understand it at all,"

Suzanne's husband said.

"Something to do with women's bio-electric field?" suggested Layla's husband.

"We need to do more tests."

"We can't tell the navy it needs to crew all its destroyers with women."

"They'll cancel the project."

"Whoever heard of an all-female space navy? It's damned ridiculous!"

Kristin took umbrage at this last comment. "Why is it ridiculous?" she demanded. "We can fight as well as men. Women have fought throughout history."

"The Amazons," put in Suzanne.

"The Valkyries," added Kristin.

"Onna-bugeisha," said Aiko.

"Queen Zenobia," said Layla.

"And it's always been visible to you?" Kristin's husband asked, quickly changing the subject.

The wives nodded.

"Even when we can't see it?" said Aiko's husband.

Despite their insistence the UESS *Aldridge* had remained stubbornly visible to them the entire time, the men seemed reluctant to believe their wives.

At that moment, Betty strolled up. She was wearing her usual flightsuit and had plainly landed minutes before from a test flight. "Hey, what's going on?" she asked the men.

Suzanne's husband quickly filled her in. As soon as she heard the UESS *Aldridge* had actually vanished from sight, she laughed. Then she said, "I watched you as I flew in. The spaceship has been here all along."

"You didn't see her disappear?"

Betty shook her head.

"So you can see the ship even when it's invisible? Just like our wives can?"

Betty nodded and grinned.

Kristin leaned in close to Suzanne. "Just think," she said, The spaceships are only invisible with women crews. And they're only invisible to men. It looks like men might be finally out of the war game."

"Oh no," said Suzanne, feeling truly happy for the first time since her husband had been assigned to the spaceyard. "If they need us to wage war, I'm sure we can find a better way to sort things out than fighting." ★

—))—

Chapter 6
First Stage Separation

In August 1967, the Eckhardts move into their new house in El Lago. Ginny is glad to get out of the apartment, but the prospect of keeping such a large house clean is daunting. It's not as if she were the most house-proud housewife in Houston, and Walden has never been particularly fussy, but they have neighbours now, other members of the astronaut corps and AWC—not just Charlie and Dotty, or Stu and Joan, from their own group, the New Nineteen, but also families from the Original Seven, the New Nine and the Fourteen.

And they might drop in or pop over at any time.

The rest of the year passes in a blur of cleaning and polishing, parties, AWC meetings, visits to the beauty parlour, keeping up appearances, keeping everything primly stable. Walden is there only at weekends, sometimes he's in Long Island at the Grumman plant, as he's now specialising in the lunar module, sometimes he's away on a geology field trip, maybe at the Grand Canyon; but mostly he's at the Cape. The Hermes Baby sits unused in a closet, there is never enough time to get it out and start writing, there is never enough time to *think* about what to write. Ginny is even struggling to keep up with her science fiction magazine reading, and she seriously considers letting some of her subscriptions lapse. She has no one to talk to about science fiction, the other wives they only read *McCall's* and *Ladies Home Journal* and *Good Housekeeping* and *Cosmopolitan* and *Redbook*. She looks at herself and she's turning into one of those robot wives. She wonders how the other wives cope, they seem so self-assured, so organised—a complaint echoed by Mary Irwin in her autobiography, *The Moon is Not Enough*, "All the other astronaut wives were in the same predicament, but they seemed to be taking it in stride. Or was it that gold-plated image we were encased in and mortally afraid of tarnishing?" Ginny must tread a careful path between the expectations of the public, the bidding of NASA, and peer pressure.

But then 'The Spaceships Men Don't See' appears in the February 1968 issue of *Galaxy*, alongside stories by Kit Reed, Kate Wilhelm, Jane Beauclerk, Gertrude Friedberg and Sydney J Van Scyoc. The response to the story is positive. Ginny receives approving letters from many of her friends, and it's enough to motivate her into finally writing all those replies she owes. But seeing the words of her story in the magazine also has a salutary effect on Ginny: she realises she needs to do more than simply keep house if she is to hold onto her sanity here in Togethersville. Being an astronaut wife is not enough, and each passing day Ginny, although not a drinker, has found herself thinking more and more about the drinks cabinet—and she won't be the first astronaut wife to fall victim to it. She remembers her conversation with Evelyn over 'The Spaceships Men Don't See' and it occurs to her she could take more of an interest in her husband's endeavours. Not simply support him, as a wife should, she's been doing that since she moved to Houston, but make an effort to understand what he's been going through, to better sympathise with the stress he's under, the strain he faces each day. After all, space travel interests her, it always has done, and here she is on the periphery of the greatest space program the planet has ever known. She knows bits and pieces, she's sneaked occasional looks at NASA press kits, but she wants to be closer still, to actually *touch* a real spacecraft, a LM or a CM, maybe even a Saturn V.

So she approaches Walden one evening:

We have the house how we want it now, Ginny says, do you think I'd be allowed to see inside the Manned Spacecraft Center?

Allowed? replies Walden. Sure, you want me to take you

round?

You can do that?

Sure, Walden assures her offhandedly.

And the Cape, I'd like to see that too, the launch pad and everything.

Hey, small steps, hon, Walden says. I'll take you in one day next week for a tour of the MSC, how about it?

It takes him several reminders before he eventually arranges something. On the day, Ginny drives to the MSC around mid-morning. The guard on the gate has obviously been informed and waves her straight through. She directs the Impala to where she's been told to park, and soon spots a figure in a pale blue flight jacket striding across the lot toward her. Even from this distance, even in clothing much like that worn by all the astronauts, she can tell from the way he moves it's her husband. Once Walden reaches her, he looks her up and down, vetting her appearance, although he has made no mention of a dress code. But what she has chosen she thinks he won't criticise, a double-breasted dress, belted, with pleated skirt, in a nice sober blue, and matching heels. She's even wearing gloves, white cotton ones, she hasn't worn a pair since she was a teenager, though she has seen other wives in gloves on their way to church on a Sunday.

You look nice, says Walden—but it's perfunctory.

He doesn't even peck her on the cheek, just turns about and heads back toward the nine-storey building from which he came. She trots after him, walking faster than normal to keep up. She wonders what's wrong, why this treatment, but as they step inside the building she sees Walden appears neither vexed nor impatient nor annoyed. He is smiling, he looks confident, he looks at ease.

This way, hon, he says.

He walks beside her, perhaps a pace or two in front, he doesn't hold her, he doesn't touch her, but he still seems to possess her. She can feel it like a forcefield extending about her, warding off all curiosity—because she is Mrs Walden J

74

Eckhardt. At times like this she wishes Virginia G Parker were not a secret, she's sure a male science fiction writer, though there are only a handful of them, would have been given VIP treatment.

What building is this? Ginny asks. Engaging her husband in conversation, she hopes, might slow his pace.

Administration, he replies.

How many buildings are there?

Hell if I know. Twenty, twenty-five, I guess.

Where are we going?

They exit the rear of the Administration Building, back out into the sunlight. Ginny stumbles, taken by surprise—she's heard the MSC described as a campus, and she's imagined something like her alma mater, SDSU, a tightly-packed complex of inter-connected buildings and small dark courtyards. Not this great park like a golf course, with three irregular lakes, scattered trees and low rolling hills of grass. Lined about its circumference are white office blocks, most no more than two or three storeys tall, and some buildings which resemble hangars or large storage sheds with blank aluminum sides and flat roofs.

Walden has halted at the abrupt double-tap of Ginny's heels on the asphalt path, and looks back at her. She gives him a wan smile and says, It's very pleasant.

Walden shrugs. Mission Control Center first, he tells her.

She can see his heart is not in this tour, perhaps he hoped she'd forget her request. But she knows some of the other wives have been to the MSC, have seen what it takes to put their husbands into space, keep them alive up there, and then bring them back safely to Earth. She thinks she knows what to expect, she's seen photographs of the MCC, although she can't remember where. Not in any of her science fiction magazines—though they may support the space program, the fact it's a wholly male undertaking rankles with the magazines' chiefly female readerships.

Ginny has seen as much in letter columns, a kind of reverse snobbery which suggests the imaginary space missions of science fiction fans are somehow a greater achievement than actually putting a man on the Moon—

And Walden ushers Ginny into a shed-like building, along a corridor and through a door—there was a sign on it, but she didn't manage to read it—and she finds herself standing in a viewing gallery at the back of a room the size of a high school gym. But it's not filled with ropes and benches, or young men in vests and shorts running back and forth between a pair of baskets... There are instead eight lines of large consoles, four to either side of a central aisle, and they're stepped so all have a good view of the five giant screens on the opposite wall. Half a dozen people sit at each of the consoles, and they're all men, all young, in short-sleeved white shirts and sombre ties and spectacles, and she just knows every one of them is an engineer, they *look* like engineers. What's that phrase Walden uses, Ginny thinks; and then as it comes to her she puts a hand to her mouth to hide a snort of laughter: "pencil-necks". Those guys there, they're pencil-necks. Walden and the other astronauts seem to hold them in some small contempt—and some not so small respect too, because they know their lives are in their hands.

Wow, says Ginny.

She steps down to the window and peers this way and that, puts a gloved hand up to the glass, and she's staring at the consoles, trying to make out what the scrolling lines of white-on-black numbers on the monitors might mean, she's marvelling at the thick manuals splayed open or piled on every surface, she's impressed by the earnestness and confidence with which these pencil-necks operate their screens and buttons and switches.

Something about the Mission Control Center strikes Ginny as bizarrely familiar, and it's a moment before she figures out what: one-upmanship. It seems to seep through the glass, a miasma of intellectual Darwinism, it's there to see in the desperate way the engineers grab manuals and point out something on a page, the urgency with which they scribble notes and calculations, the need for approval evident in every bespectacled gaze in the MCC. It's nothing like the testosterone which coloured the air at Edwards, or perhaps it's a less potent version of it, but there is still a sense that not only do these engineers know they're the best at what they do but they also feel an addict's compulsion to demonstrate it time and time again.

Walden walks down to join her at the glass, and Ginny abruptly realises most of the men in the MCC have turned about and are now staring at her as if they've never seen a woman before. She feels Walden slide an arm around her waist and she gives an abashed smile, looks to her husband, back again into the MCC... and sees the pencil-necks' gazes have now shifted to Walden—and from their expressions alone Ginny knows that her husband is *an astronaut*.

Is there anything happening? she asks him.

She's beginning to feel like an exhibit in a zoo, one of a mating pair of exotic animals when, really, she's the one on the *outside* looking *in*.

Walden makes a face. There's an unmanned flight of the Apollo stack scheduled for next month, he tells her, so they can man-rate the Saturn V.

That's the one that's going to take you to the Moon?

He manhandles her about, none too gently, and with a hand to the small of her back, directs her up the steps to the exit from the gallery. Out in the corridor, she pulls away from him, and she can sense him simmering.

Not me, he snaps. I'm just one of the greenhorns, I've not even been asked to support a flight.

I'm sure you'll get your chance, she assures him. But she knows the words are empty, as does he, her sympathy won't get him what he desires most. She's doing her best, she's been trying so hard, just look at the way she's dressed, she goes to the beauty parlour regularly, she attends the AWC meetings and stays on good terms with all the other wives.

This way, Walden says brusquely. And he's off again down the corridor.

Another building, another gym-sized room. This, explains Walden, is the Apollo Lunar Mission Simulator. There are banks and banks of computers, with flashing lights and reels of tape that abruptly zip clockwise then anticlockwise. There is a great cubical frame of steel girders off to one side, and just visible within it is a grey and cratered diorama. And there are the three simulators, which look like someone opened a giant closet and all the boxes inside just fell out into piles. Walden points over at a large U-shaped console which looks up at one of the simulators.

That's where the pencil-necks set up the mission parameters, he tells her. It's all computerised.

There's a lot of computers, Ginny says.

Yeah, 4.2 million bucks' worth.

It's a sum beyond imagining for Ginny, though not, she suspects, inconceivable to those closely involved with Apollo—after all, putting a man into space, putting *a man on the Moon*, is a hugely expensive endeavour.

This way, says Walden. This is the LM simulator.

He takes Ginny's arm and leads her up a short flight of red-carpeted stairs to a platform at the back of the piles of boxes, and he steps through an entranceway into the simulator itself. Ginny halts at the jamb and peers in, and she can feel her pulse quicken as she takes in the grey panels of switches and dials and readouts, the two tiny triangular windows, the hand controllers—and it all looks so very *real*, an actual spacecraft, something that's designed to operate in space, to land on the surface of another world. Cold fingers run up her spine and she thinks about magazine and book covers and descriptions in prose in short stories and novellas and novels, about spaceship bridges and control rooms, and here she is gazing at a tiny cabin which will carry two men to the Moon, and *in no way* does it resemble anything her imagination might have created from the science fiction she has read over the years. She looks down at her feet and wonders if she should

```
        FLIGHT CONTROL DIVISION
          Subcourse Outline

COURSE:        Lunar Module Cockpit Simulation
               Trainer
SUBCOURSE:     LM        Crew        Compartment
Familiarization
               Phase I A
TYPE OF
INSTRUCTION:   Practical Exercise
TIME ALLOTTED: Approximately 30 minutes
REFERENCES:    Apollo Operations Handbook

     LM CREW COMPARTMENT FAMILIARIZATION
                 PHASE I A

   Phase I A of LM cockpit simulation training
is an introductory session concerned with the
physical layout of the crew compartment, crew
controls and displays and general spacecraft
systems functions. Only general systems control
areas will be pointed out in this phase of
training. Upon completion of this phase, you
will be capable of locating all major controls
and displays within the crew compartment.
   A projection screen is located in the
commander's forward window as an aid to location
of specific items within the crew compartment.
```

take off her heels, they might damage the lunar module, she's heard it is fragile, walls as thin as a beercan's—but this, of course, is just a simulator, and the floor is good and solid. So she steps inside beside her husband and he tells her she's at the commander's position. She grabs a hand controller with each gloved hand and she stares through the window, which is really some kind of screen, at the surface of the Moon, which is really the diorama she saw earlier inside the giant steel framework. Now she's starting to feel a little faint, she might even swoon, the sheer *physicality* of this tiny spacecraft cabin, of the grey instrument panels on every available surface, the dials, the switches, the digital readouts, the little blue and black ball bobbing this way and that beneath a glass etched with reticulations, and everything carefully labelled, so meticulously labelled. Her husband could be going to the Moon, she thinks. She knows this, she's known it for two years now. (Of course, he might never get selected for a flight—there are sixty-one of them now, and not enough missions for all.) Until this moment, it has never quite struck her precisely what this means. Ginny has read science fiction for much of her life, she calls herself a fan, she has written letters to the magazines, she writes stories, many of the science fiction authors whose books she sees in book stores, she considers friends. But it all means nothing when confronted with this. Sense of wonder, imagination, pictures painted with the mind's eye, it all pales into insignificance, seems to flatten to two dimensions like some painted backdrop, a theatrical flat, when compared to this reality, to Apollo, the lunar module, this machine which will put two astronauts—and one of them could be her husband!—on the surface of an alien planet.

Walden is speaking: See, we fly the LM down from lunar orbit to the surface, it's mostly all done by the pings but we might have to take over for the last few feet.

Ginny has recovered from her near-fainting fit. She turns to her husband and says, Pings? Like they have in submarines?

But no, that can't be right—there's no air in space, so there's no sound, Ginny knows that much.

Pings, says Walden, P-G-N-C-S, Primary Guidance, Navigation and Control System.

So how does that work? she asks. Explain it to me, like you would to another astronaut.

Another astronaut? asks Walden.

You know what I mean. She grins—and adds, I love it when you talk dirty.

It is intended to be a joke, a lightening of the mood, though this cramped cabin with its grey instrument panels doesn't lend itself to frivolity.

Walden evidently feels that way: Dirty? It's *technical*, Ginny.

Tell me about the switches and these things—what do you call these things?

Barber poles.

And this? What's this? she asks and presses idly on the number-pad. Verb? she asks. Noun?

Diskey, he tells her.

She looks at him, not understanding.

He spells it out: D S K Y—Display Keyboard. We call it the diskey.

What's it for?

Programming the guidance computer, he tells her.

And all these switches?

Jeez, Ginny, you want me to explain every one we'll be here all day.

What's these ones? Ascent He, Descent He. What's He?

The moment she says it, she figures out that "He" is helium, but she says nothing as Walden replies:

The fuel for the rocket engines has to be kept pressurised, so we use helium because it's inert.

Ginny may have studied Lit at SDSU, but she knows what helium is.

The fuel for the engines is hypergolic, Walden adds.

There's a relish to the way he says "hypergolic", like it's a secret word, the password to some secret club. Ginny doesn't know what it means, why should she? Yet she can think of plenty of words Walden could not define, and not just ones like "camisole" or "pleat", but even scientific terms she has come across during her years of reading science fiction, such as "parsec" and "semantics". She even knows what the Fermi Paradox is, and she's pretty sure

Walden has no idea.

Hypergolic, he explains, means the two fuels ignite as soon as they mix. We don't need to burn them, like on the Saturn V.

They should use women as astronauts, we're smaller, says Ginny, we'd use less fuel, we even use less oxygen, less water, less food.

It takes more than that, hon. It takes years of training, of flying jet fighters.

So flying a spacecraft is like flying a jet fighter?

Well, no, not really, I guess.

So why do astronauts need to be jet fighter pilots?

It's complicated.

Walden, you can't even cook a roast dinner, and you're telling me being an astronaut is too complicated for a woman?

Women could never be astronauts, he insists. It's just the way it is.

She doesn't know it, but Ginny's point has already been proven—as I have written elsewhere in another work of fiction. In August 1961, Dr W Randolph Lovelace II gave a talk at a symposium of aerospace scientists in Stockholm in which he declared women better suited as astronauts, based on the medical testing he had given to female pilot Geraldyne M Cobb. "We are already in a position to say that certain qualities of the female space pilot are preferable to those of her male colleague," he told his audience. Cobb's testing was in all the newspapers, and covered extensively by *Life* magazine—but Ginny's journey of discovery, her exploration into making use of her husband's profession in her science fiction writing, requires her to be ignorant of the Mercury 13. And so the Eckhardts were in Germany at that time, and Ginny's chief link with home was her science fiction magazines. Which, for some reason, made no mention of it, a lack of sisterly solidarity that might be considered uncharacteristic, although perhaps the magazines' readerships mostly felt, as Jackie Cochran did when she testified before a Congressional subcommittee against a women's astronaut program, that it was men's job to lead the way and for women to follow on and "pick up the slack".

And isn't that what Ginny is doing? Letting her man lead the way. Of course she's not qualified to be an astronaut—

Dear Mr. Pohl,

V. G. Parker's February story, "The Spaceships Men Don't See" deserves some comments on its frankly bizarre approach to telling what could have been a sound and ingenious piece of science fiction. Much as we may love them, wives have no place in serious science fiction. Or, if they must appear, it should be in the background, nobly supporting their men. But Mr. Parker, for reasons best known only to himself, decides that rather than science and engineering we should be presented with womanly gossip and high heels. Perhaps he thought he was being clever.

If that's his excuse, I have no idea what might be your excuse for publishing this story. Your male readers greatly outnumber your female readers, and that's a stone-cold fact. We are not in the littlest bit interested in women's affairs. If we wanted that, we would be reading a woman's magazine and not *Galaxy*.

Robert Allman
4597 Seaview Ave.
Tampa, Fla. 33611

---

she watches her weight and tries to exercise, but she's no athlete; and she cannot fly an airplane, there is only one licenced pilot in the AWC, and that's Trudy.

But now that Ginny considers it, as she stands inside the lunar module simulator, it occurs to her that while she can never become an astronaut herself there's no reason why she can't write about them. Not something like Judith's story about the tramp spaceship with the male doctor in an otherwise all-female crew, a story that has been a perennial favourite since its original appearance a decade before. No, Ginny is thinking of something much closer to home, a space program much like Mercury, Gemini and Apollo, those first faltering steps into space... but by women.

The more she thinks about it, the more she likes the idea. She has access to much of the material Walden is using in his training, she can probably get hold of some press kits, and she can use it for research, for the background to her stories. And the more she finds out, the more she understands what an astronaut is and does, the more she will be a better partner to Walden, understand his frustrations, emotionally support him.

It doesn't occur to her until later that perhaps Walden will object to Ginny "interfering" in his area of expertise. He is the astronaut in the family, she is the wife. As a military man, Walden has always been keen on well-defined areas of responsibility—his den is out of bounds, her dressing-room is of no interest to him; the mess he makes it is her job to tidy up, any mess she might make is, of course, her job to clean up...

They exit the LM simulator and as Ginny stands at the top of the steps, she asks, Are they the same? The other two simulators?

They're command modules, Walden replies.

Oh, can I see inside one of those?

Walden glances across at the LM simulator console, there's a lone pencil-neck with his head down, busy doing something, programming perhaps. I guess, Walden says.

But the CM simulator is accessed via a steep ladder leading up to a hatch in the side of the cone-shaped spacecraft. There's no way Ginny can climb that in her high-heeled pumps, so she slips them off, hands them to Walden, and starts up the ladder. She looks back over her shoulder, and there are a couple of guys over at one of the computer banks and they're gazing in her direction, so she puts a hand to her skirt to keep it pressed against the back of her legs. It's an inelegant scramble to get through the hatch and inside the CM, and it's such a cramped space in there, she can't believe three grown men—in spacesuits!—will fly to the Moon in it, even she has to duck her head. She works her way round to where three seats in a row gaze up at a wide instrument panel covered in switches and dials and meters and barber poles; and there's the diskey, recognising it makes her smile. But just then she feels something catch her calf, and she looks down and says, Oh shoot. She has snagged her nylons on something and now there's a run up one leg from the heel to the back of her knee. She can't be seen around the MSC like that, so she hikes up her skirt, slips her fingers under the waistband of her pantyhose—

Jeez, Ginny!

It's Walden, filling the hatchway.

What the hell are you doing?

She peels off her hose, an awkward manoeuvre in the tight space, scrunches it up and passes it to her husband, asking, Can you put this in your pocket?

On the way back to the parking lot, Walden and Ginny bump into Al Shepard, the first American into space. She's heard the stories about the "icy commander" but they must have caught him on a good day, he is charm itself, shaking Walden's hand vigorously, flashing a boyish grin at Ginny, maybe even flirting with her a little.

Afterward, Ginny can't help saying, Fancy meeting Alan Shepard, a real astronaut!

I'm a real astronaut too, protests Walden.

She hugs his arm with both hands and pecks him on the cheek. Sorry, darling, she tells him, I just meant he's been into space; but you will too, Walden, I know you will.

But she's thinking about someone else going into space, someone who is not real.

—☽—

Chapter 7
Lunar Transfer Injection

Soon after, Walden is invited to join the support crew for the Apollo 10 mission, which is the one that will be going to the Moon but not actually landing on it. There is some sort of rota which NASA uses to determine who flies when and on which mission. Because Walden has been picked for a support crew, he thinks the chances are good he will get an actual flight. Or so he tells Ginny. Tom picked him for this support crew, that's evidence of Tom's confidence in his abilities, Walden is sure of it. For Ginny, it makes more real the prospect of her husband going to the Moon, and while before she felt proud and honoured, now she begins to feel a little bit afraid.

It's not like spaceflight has proven any more dangerous than she'd imagined—Apollo 1 happened on the ground, after all; although everyone still bears the scars of the tragedy. The Soviets have lost only a single cosmonaut, Vladimir Komarov, who plummetted to the ground from orbit and scuttlebutt has it he was cursing all the way down. But Apollo 7 launches safely in October, and three guys spend ten days in orbit testing all the systems in the re-designed command module.

Ginny, accompanying Pam and Mary, drops by Loella's house, and she sits in the Cunninghams' lounge, sipping coffee, the other women also smoking cigarettes, and though Loella casts an occasional worried glance at the NASA squawk box on the dresser, the conversation mostly confines itself to gossip about the AWC. They don't talk about the Vietnam War, though they know women from their air force, navy and marine corps days whose husbands are over there fighting. They don't mention the protest in

Atlantic City against the Miss America pageant—after all, what do they have in common with those women, the protestors or the contestants? The Olympics in Mexico City, the opening ceremony was the day after the Apollo 7 launch, doesn't enter the conversation. This is the year in which both Martin Luther King Jr and Bobby Kennedy were assassinated and now, months later, neither event is ever mentioned at the AWC. Oh, there was a peace march through Houston after King's death, and the *Houston Chronicle* claimed an astronaut participated...

This is Togethersville and talk runs along well-worn rails: Apollo flights, home life, church, children... A practiced litany of domestic details with ample opportunity for sympathy, humour, boasting and envy. Ginny lets the words wash over her, there's something about Wally and Donn, the flight's not going well and the way they've been talking back to Houston, it could be the end of their careers.

Dodie, the *Life* journalist, she's with the Schirras today, so they can talk freely. They can all smell a rat in the Eisele home, but everyone knows Togethersville has more than its fair share of rodents. Ginny listens with a fixed smile on her face and she wonders if her husband is as faithless as these women claim astronauts by nature are. What else, besides the training, the swagger, the constant broadcasting of the Right Stuff, must her husband do to get a shot at the Moon? And she worries how easy it would be for Walden to get himself into a situation where he never gets a flight.

Now that Walden is supporting Apollo 10, she sees less of him than ever. He spends most of the week at the Cape, and he doesn't always fly home for the weekend. Has his behaviour changed? She can't tell, she's an Air Force wife, it's always been like this. If there is a difference now—other than the quality of housing, and the fact they actually own the property—it's this: whatever Walden is doing is in the public eye. No more military secrets. He can talk about it. He doesn't, of course; not with Ginny. But she is still bent on her plan to learn more about Walden's profession, the only thing putting a brake on it is his frequent absences.

Ginny drives home from the Cunningham house on automatic pilot. She knows about closed communities, she's lived in them for most of her life, Air Force bases and, now she thinks about it, science fiction is much the same. Though her friends are scattered about the country, and they talk via letters and the occasional telephone call, they are all just as inward-looking, as cut-off from the real world, as Togethersville.

Ginny lives in two worlds, a high-heeled pump in each, and neither world seems much interested in reality. And though both exist for pretty much the same reason, the links between them are few and weak. When she goes shopping, and she sees those meagre handfuls of science fiction paperbacks in the book stores, with their gaudy covers featuring pretty women in spacesuits, piloting spaceships or exploring alien worlds; and then over by the magazines, there's *Life*, with a Saturn V on a pillar of flame arrowing across the cover.

Are the two really so far apart?

Back at the house, Ginny kicks off her shoes, in the bedroom she strips down to her panties and bra and then, almost reverently, takes her slacks and plaid shirt from the chest of drawers. She sits on the double-bed she shares these days with Walden only on occasional weekends, and gazes down at the folded garments in her lap. It's been nearly eighteen months since she wrote 'The Spaceships Men Don't See' and though she tells herself she's been too busy to write in the months since, she knows she's blocked. She can't tell her friends, she can't mention it in her letters to Ursula, Ali, Judith, Joanna... It's a confession too far, if there's one thing the AWC has taught her it's that you only open up so much—hell, if there's one thing *marriage* has taught her, it's that some things need to remain secrets.

The truth is, she's been meaning to make good on her epiphany in the lunar module simulator eight months ago, but every time she sneaks a look at one of Walden's training manuals the scale of the task she has set herself overwhelms her. So she goes and cleans the bathroom. Or she calls up Mary or Louise or Dotty. Or she does a million and one other things that are not writing science fiction or trying to learn how an Apollo spacecraft functions. She has been co-opted, assimilated: she has become *an astronaut wife.*

It's not how Ginny sees herself, not inside, it's a part she has been playing, that's all. These slacks, this plaid shirt, they're the real Virginia Grace Eckhardt née Parker. It was so easy to be her, back in those days at Edwards, of ceramic blue skies and desert heat and that fine layer of dust which settled on every surface, living miles from anywhere; science fiction was a lifeline, one she clung to with a desperation born of despair. But, oh, how easily she has been corrupted by this new life gifted her by NASA, by that shining beacon in the night sky—which, for the first time in the history of Man, it's become possible to visit.

Ginny dresses quickly, almost feverishly. She gets an old pair of sandals out of the closet. She fetches her Hermes Baby, and a stack of typing paper, from her dressing-room, and carries them reverently into the lounge. It is late afternoon, she has a lonely evening stretching ahead of her, normally she'd make herself a salad or something light and then curl up in front of the television, maybe with a magazine to read.

Not tonight. She makes herself a scotch, with plenty of water, not the iced tea which used to fuel her when she was writing, and she sits at the table and holds her hands in readiness over the keys—

Something about going to the Moon, she's going to write a story about a mission to the Moon. And she's going to make it accurate and full of realistic detail, a new sort of science fiction, rigorous and backed up by real science and engineering.

A cynical reader might observe Ginny's evolving relationship to science fiction, and it's not the science fiction we know, as illustrated by the names of the published writers, all of which are real science fiction authors, which have been mentioned in this novel—Ginny's changing thoughts and dreams on, and of, the genre, as influenced by her husband's new career, by this great new adventure the USA is undertaking, recapitulate this quartet's relationship to science fiction. It would be disingenuous to claim this is happenstance—Ginny is a fictional construct and her life created toward a particular end. And a particular resolution. But there is a wider point to make here: "motif" and "theme" are synonyms for "pattern", and human beings are predisposed to find patterns, even where they do not exist. It takes little to suggest a higher purpose at work—some carefully-placed hints, an element of serendipity, an insistence that some of the topics explored by literature are universal...

Ginny has learnt for herself that "universal" is not quite so all-encompassing a term the dictionary definition claims. Critical studies of science fiction are almost non-existent: perhaps some Lit student somewhere has written a thesis on the fiction of Margaret St Clair or Alice Norton, but Ginny does not know of any. Science fiction is genre fiction, women's fiction, not deemed worthy of study. And men control the literature departments of American universities, Ginny knows this for herself (nothing has changed since she graduated). Male professors are not interested in fiction read and written by women.

And yet... Ginny looks down at her hands poised over the typewriter keys, and considers what she is about to do. She is going to take an endeavour which has been presented to the world as the very pinnacle of male achievement—for all of Betty Skelton's accomplishments, it is only men who have the "Right Stuff"—and she is going to colonise, no, *occupy* it, in the name of women. She is going to take from men something they have quite deliberately kept for themselves—and it is by no means the only such thing—and she is going to re-invent it for her gender...

The audacity of her plan intimidates her.

Lunar Module (LM)

The lunar module is a two-stage vehicle designed
for space operations near and on the Moon. The
lunar module stands 22 feet 11 inches high and is
31 feet wide (diagonally across landing gear). The
ascent and descent stages of the LM operate as a
unit until staging, when the ascent stage functions
as a single spacecraft for rendezvous and docking
with the CM.

Ascent Stage--Three main sections make up the
ascent stage: the crew compartment, midsection, and
aft equipment bay. Only the crew compartment and
midsection are pressurized (4.8 psig). The cabin
volume is 235 cubic feet (6.7 cubic meters). The
stage measures 12 feet 4 inches high by 14 feet 1
inch in diameter. The ascent stage has six
substructural areas: crew compartment, midsection,
aft equipment bay, thrust chamber assembly cluster
supports, antenna supports, and thermal and
micrometeroid shield.

The cylindrical crew compartment is 92 inches
(2.35 meters) in diameter and 42 inches (1.07
meters) deep. Two flight stations are equipped with
control and display panels, arm-rests, body-
restraints, landing aids, two front windows, an
overhead docking window, and an alignment optical
  telescope in the center between the two flight
stations. The habitable volume is 160 cubic feet.

A tunnel ring atop the ascent stage meshes with
the command module docking latch assemblies. During
docking, the CM docking ring and latches are
aligned by the LM drogue and the CSM probe.

The docking tunnel extends downwards into the
midsection 16 inches (40 cm). The tunnel is 32
inches (81 cm) in diameter and is used for crew
transfer between the CSM and LM. The upper hatch on
the inboard end of the docking tunnel opens inward
and cannot be opened without equalizing pressure on
both hatch surfaces.

A thermal and micrometeoroid shield of multiple
layers of Mylar and a single thickness of thin

aluminum skin encases the entire ascent stage structure.

Descent Stage--The descent stage center compartment houses the descent engine, and descent propellant tanks are housed in the four bays around the engine. Quadrant II contains ALSEP. The radioisotope thermoelectric generator (RTG) is externally mounted. Quadrant IV contains the MESA. The descent stage measure ten feet seven inches high by 14 feet 1 inch in diameter and is enclosed in the Mylar and aluminum alloy thermal and micrometeoroid shield. The LRV is stowed in Quadrant I.

The LM egress platform or "porch" is mounted on the forward outrigger just below the forward hatch. A ladder extends down the forward landing gear strut from the porch for crew lunar surface operations.

The landing gear struts are released explosively and are extended by springs. They provide lunar surface landing impact attenuation. The main struts are filled with crushable aluminum honeycomb for absorbing compression loads. Footpads 37 inches (0.95 m) in diameter at the end of each landing gear provide vehicle support on the lunar surface.

Each pad (except forward pad) is fitted with a 68-inch long lunar surface sensing probe which upon contact with the lunar surface signals the crew to shut down the descent engine.

The Apollo LM has a launch weight of 36,230 pounds. The weight breakdown is as follows:

Ascent stage, dry	4,690 lbs.	Includes water and
Descent stage, dry	6,179 lbs.	oxygen; no crew
RCS propellants (loaded)	633 lbs.	
DPS propellants (loaded)	19,508 lbs.	
APS propellants (loaded)	5,220 lbs.	

	36,230 lbs.	

Ginny's empty promise earlier in the year proves prophetic when Walden is chosen for the Apollo 12 backup crew by Dave Scott. The rotation schedule means he will get to fly on Apollo 15—David Scott, Commander; Alfred Worden, Command Module Pilot; Walden Eckhardt, Lunar Module Pilot. An all Air Force crew—not just their friend and neighbour back in California, Al; but Dave was also at Edwards when he was selected by NASA in 1963 (the Eckhardts knew of him back then but they did not socialise).

NASA makes the announcement about Apollo 12 in April of 1969, and while all the attention is rightly directed at Pete Conrad, Al Bean and Dick Gordon, the Apollo 12 prime crew, a few weekends after the press release, Ginny and Walden are invited to Dave and Lurton's ranch-style home in Nassau Bay for a celebration. Al is there, but not Pam, the two have been separated for about six months—and there are some in the Astronaut Wives Club who feel that should make Al ineligible for a flight, they've stuck by their men through thick and thin, good and bad, they have made *sacrifices*, and Pam has let them all down. But Ginny is not one of them. She was sad to see Pam leave, she always liked her, they were friends, if not especially close ones—Ginny's closest friends she has never actually met in person, they're the people she corresponds with and whose names she sees in the pages of the magazines she reads.

Back in Edwards, everyone partied hard, but the mantle of responsibility laid across the astronauts' shoulders by the nation has left them subdued and more inclined to work off their frustrations in the privacy of their own homes. For Ginny, this has meant fights, nights where Walden silently and sullenly chugs beer, the two of them occasionally sleeping in separate bedrooms and reproachful apologies the following morning. She knows Walden is under pressure, that the work is hard—she is trying herself to understand what NASA is asking of him... although she has not yet worked up the courage to tell him so.

Dave has been in space twice before, on Gemini 8 and Apollo 9, and Walden has admitted to her he couldn't have asked for a better commander. The Apollo 11 crew were later described by Michael Collins as "amiable strangers", but the Apollo 15 crew are as close as long-time colleagues. Tied together by shared memories of Edwards, by careers that have trod similar paths, they are alike enough to be comfortable in each other's presence, and yet different enough not to cavil at their enforced closeness. In *Falling to Earth*, Al Worden describes Dave Scott as "the quintessential professional", Jim Irwin as "restrained and reticent" and Scott's "yes-man"; and in reference to his own role: "[Scott] wanted things his way, but on a few occasions I had to tell him, 'Well, Dave, I am not sure I want to do it like that.'" The crew had, in Worden's words, "a bond of competence and professionalism". Imagine a similar dynamic at play with Walden J Eckhardt in Jim Irwin's place. When Walden's conversation becomes peppered with "Dave" and "Al", Ginny is at first glad everything seems to be going so well; but it soon palls. She looks forward to the days when Walden is at the Cape, and she will not be sharing the bed with her husband and the ghosts of his crew-mates.

The Scotts' party takes the form of a luau, though neither Ginny nor Walden have been to Hawaii and so can't vouch for its authenticity. The shirts are certainly Hawaiian—the Scotts have provided suitable garments for Al and Walden. And there are pineapples and a barbecue with far too much meat. Ginny is no stranger to barbecues, they were regular occurrences at Edwards, but there is something desperately festive about this one. It's not just the ridiculous paper leis, or the paper lanterns strung across the garden, or even the cake with the Moon drawn in blue icing on its top.

Ginny sits alone at a table, in a plain red top and white capri pants—her concession to the theme, though several of the other wives are in muumuus, but now she thinks about it maybe they wore capri pants in *Girls! Girls! Girls!* and not

Blue Hawaii—and sips from some fruity cocktail which boasts a pair of swizzle sticks and a paper umbrella, Lurton told her the name but she can't remember it. And she's thinking about the short story she finished a few days ago, the third since she discovered how to write again, the third since she started to make good on her epiphany in the LM simulator all those months ago, the third since she's been working her way secretly through her husband's training manuals. Not all of the stories have worked, often some vital narrative element seems just beyond her grasp, and the one she has sent out has not sold, the rejections sadly uninformative on the story's flaws.

Hey, why so glum, asks Dave, as he marches past bearing a huge bowl of potato salad.

Ginny starts. Uh, I was a million miles away, she tells him. She considers adding she was in fact only a quarter of a million miles from Houston, Texas, somewhere in the vicinity of the Sea of Tranquility, designated Apollo Landing Site 1. But he has already swept past.

Apollo 11 will actually land at Apollo Landing Site 2, also in the Sea of Tranquility, but some 150 miles west of Site 1. Ginny cannot know this, of course, not in April 1969, as NASA has not yet announced where the first lunar landing will take place.

She watches Dave bear down on the table at the other end of the patio and begin sorting the plates and dishes on its top to find room for the potato salad. Although the food has been made by the wives, the men always take charge during a barbecue, presenting the various dishes as if they themselves were responsible for the salads and sauces and condiments.

A hand settles on her shoulder and Ginny looks up to see a man smiling down at her. He is wearing aviator sunglasses and has a bottle of beer in one hand. For one brief moment, she wonders who he is—and is thrown into even more confusion when Dave turns and yells, Hey, Swede!

Swede? Ginny asks her husband.

It's nothing, hon, says Walden, just a dumb nickname.

He walks away. She can hear the chatter of the other wives behind her, busy doing something inside the house, and now the men have congregated at the barbecue, leaving Ginny alone and between the two groups. She should be indoors, joining in the gossip, helping with the food preparation which remains to be done, she's a fully paid up member of the AWC and she's been in it now for two and a half years. But she sits at the table by herself and thinks about the future.

Not just the future of the here-and-now, Walden backup crew for Apollo 12, which is due to fly later this year, but also Walden prime crew for an upcoming flight to the Moon. And because he has specialised in the lunar module, has spent the last eighteen months studying it, because it is *his* spacecraft, so he is LMP, which means he will certainly be setting foot on the lunar surface. But there is also the future of Ginny's invented worlds—and there's that famous story of Judith's which opens, "Martha begat Joan and Joan begat Ariadne. Ariadne lived and died at home on Pluto, but her daughter, Emma, took the long trip out to a distant planet of an alien sun". But who needs an alien sun when there's an alien world hanging over everyone's head, and the more Ginny learns of the science and engineering of putting a man on the Moon, the more she realises how astonishingly *difficult* a task it is, and the freedom of the galaxy, as practiced by her friends and peers, seems a thing so very fanciful, so much more so than imagining a woman walking through lunar regolith—and that's something she supposes will never come to pass.

The wives spill out into the garden, in their vibrantly-coloured muumuus and dresses, and the men mill about with their bottles of beer, and Ginny sits alone in the centre of what feels like a whirlwind of activity, as if time has slowed for her, everyone moving so fast, their voices an unintelligible gabble, and the irony of her situation, that she, someone who travels forward in time in her stories, does not escape her.

And then Walden is looming over her and she puts her empty glass on the table and rises to her feet, tottering a moment on her high-heeled mules. The sun is sinking, spraying reds and oranges across the darkening sky, like fire splashing over a launch pad as a Saturn 1B lifts off, not that Ginny has seen one in person, only some footage on television and photographs in magazines. She smiles at her husband as he snakes an arm about her waist and pulls her in close, and this is the most intimate he has been in over a year— No, not "intimate", he has been that, their sex life has suffered but it still limps along. This is the most *husbandly* he has been since they moved to Houston— holding her close, and she knows she loves him for all his faults, and she knows he reciprocates the feeling in his own way, and looking across to the other astronauts and their wives, she thinks, what an extraordinary group of people we are and what an extraordinary time this is to live. The things we are doing here in Houston, in just a few short months we will put a human being on the Moon—and the *realness* of it is palpable, is there to be felt in the muscular arm encircling her waist, in the warmth of Walden's body pressed against her own, in the drunken gestures and bright chatter, the toothsome smiles and wholesome features. There's such a sense of community to this gathering, one that science fiction, for all its decades of stories and letter columns has never quite managed.

She thinks perhaps it's because science fiction fans don't get together, they don't meet up, their husbands likely wouldn't allow it, fathers would certainly not let teenage daughters travel to other cities alone to visit other science fiction fans. Maybe there are small literary circles dedicated to science fiction at some universities, perhaps some of them even have male members... But fandom as such, it can't even decide on an award, they've been discussing it since the late fifties, but who to name it for? Francis Stevens? She was prolific and popular during the first two decades of the century, she arguably invented science fiction; but perhaps they should use her real name, Gertrude Burrows Bennett? Or, how about a long-established and successful living author? Alice Norton? Catherine Moore? And there were those writers who were successful back in the 1930s, just as the science fiction magazines began to appear, like Leslie F Stone and Claire Winger Harris and Hazel Heald...

Lurton rushes up and holds out a hand for Ginny, and she's pulled from her husband's side and over to a group of wives, and someone pushes another cocktail into her hand, and as she hears the topic of conversation—it's Togethersville gossip, of course, divorces and separations, but it's also about the upcoming Apollo 11 and Neil, standing over there by the barbecue, he's going to be *the first man to set foot on the Moon*... Janet doesn't know whether to be proud or frightened, and so settles for both, and though Janet and Lurton are firm friends, no one really knows Neil, who is often almost inhumanly distant—so much so David Scott mistakenly ascribes to him Pete Conrad's motto, "if you can't be good, be colourful", in the autobiography Scott shares with Alexei Leonov, *Two Sides of the Moon*.

And it all brings Ginny abruptly back to Earth and it's a rapid enough descent to make her head spin. Which she blames on the drink, as she puts a hand up to her mouth and gives a sheepish grin.

—)—

Chapter 8
Lunar Orbit Insertion

Nineteen sixty-nine is a red letter year, the year a man first sets foot on the Moon, the year NASA, the people of the United States of America, make good on their president's promise, "before this decade is out, of landing a man on the Moon and returning him safely to the Earth". Apollo 7 and Apollo 8 launched the previous year, of course—and who can forget Bill, Jim and Frank reading verses from the Book of Genesis 234,474 miles from the Earth? Apollo 9, a month before the Scotts' luau, was almost routine by comparison.

At the beginning of the decade, the Space Race was exciting, it captured the public's imagination. Alan Shepard, the first American but the second man into space, spent only fifteen minutes in a suborbital hop, he met the president, who gave him a medal. John Glenn, Scott Carpenter, Gordo Cooper, Gus Grissom, they all had ticker tape parades in New York. The Gemini flights weren't so glamorous, nothing could ever be "routine" about spaceflight, but they were no longer front page news, the astronauts who flew them didn't go on world tours. Sure, everyone had to spend some time "in the barrel", and even Walden has given talks to high schools and plant workers.

But the Apollo flights are different. America is in front, they're beating the Soviets. It puts the astronauts back in the headlines. Frank, Bill and Jim even get a ticker tape parade after their trip around the Moon.

Ginny, of course, is still pretty much a nobody—she's sort of famous because she's an astronaut wife, but Walden Jefferson Eckhardt is only one of fifty-four astronauts and he's never flown so no one is really all that eager to interview Ginny or snap photographs of her. None of the reporters, of course, know about her career as Virginia G Parker—she can just imagine the magazine articles if they ever found out.

As backup to Apollo 12's LMP, Al Bean—Ginny is aware of Pete Conrad's crew, with their matching gold and black Corvettes, but she knows the wives only in passing—Walden is at the Cape pretty much all the time. She understands he might have to take Al's place, and she'd want him as prepared as possible should such an eventuality arise... To be honest, she's used to it now, she's used to being left on her own for weeks, seeing her husband only infrequently. The house keeps her busy—my God, the endless housework—the AWC is there when she feels the need for company, and the new sense of purpose she has brought to her writing is proving the sort of intellectual challenge she now realises she has been missing. For those long busy months of 1969, as spring fades and summer threatens to throw a blanket of muggy heat over Houston, Ginny is happier than she has ever been. Though she has never thought of herself as a homemaker, she is proud of their home, proud of the hand she played in creating it; and she is beginning to enjoy her reflected minor celebrity, the wife of an astronaut who will probably go to the Moon, even if it has yet to be officially confirmed.

In May, Apollo 10 launches, and its crew of three make the quarter of a million mile journey to the Moon, and then descend to within ten miles of its surface. But they do not land. Ginny visits Faye during the flight, sitting on the sofa, trying to listen to the other women present and the squawk box at the same time. But really she wants Walden home so she can ask him to explain what is going on. She hears something over the squawk box and it sounds like: Okay, it's attitude control three mode control ... commander is four jet ... when you hit hard over here it's going to be hot fire.

But Walden is not in Houston, and though Ginny can find her way around a diagram of the lunar module, and

100

make an educated guess at some of the workings depicted in sub-system diagrams, much of the astronauts' speech is impenetrable, full of acronyms and terms she doesn't understand. What she needs is a glossary and a legend for the acronyms.

As the mission progresses, a day in orbit, three days travelling to the Moon, Ginny feels Walden's absence keenly, they should be experiencing this together, Apollo 10 validates everything that has happened since he applied to NASA, since they moved to Houston. Ginny wants to share the excitement—and not just with the other wives, whose responses are... *complicated*. Faye and the two Barbaras fear for their husbands' safety but are also proud of their achievement—every other wife is just frightened at the prospect of their own husband up there, reliant upon something built by the lowest bidder... Though they may all profess to be "proud, thrilled and happy", that's only for the sake of the press. Certainly those three sentiments are present, but they are only part of a potent rocket fuel of emotions.

I am, incidentally, indulging in some artistic licence here. In his autobiography *We Have Capture*, commander Tom Stafford makes absolutely no mention of his wife and daughters during his discussion of the Apollo 10 flight. And Lily Koppel in *The Astronaut Wives Club* skips straight from Apollo 8 to Apollo 11. But it seems to me the mission should play an important role in Ginny's journey of discovery, an almost metaphorical role—in a story in which the US space program has been put to more than its fair share of metaphorical uses...

Ginny fears for the Apollo 10 astronauts because they are using the same hardware her husband will be using when he goes to the Moon; but she is also frightened they might fail, and so the program will be cancelled and Walden will never set foot on the lunar surface. And then there's what she knows about the spacecraft... So many things that could go wrong, that could fail at any point during the mission and spell death for the crew, even with all the triple redundancies.

It's something that science fiction, now Ginny thinks about it, never really considers. Space travel is a literary device, it serves to get characters across interplanetary or interstellar distances from point A to point B, as the story requires... But in the real world such journeys are dangerous, space travel is dangerous, space is a hazardous environment, as Ginny has been learning—and science fiction all too often glosses over those facts. It's an unlooked-for disconnect and it has slowly insinuated itself into her life over the past two years, and she's not entirely sure how to deal with it.

But, at the moment, she's mostly concerned with the Walden-shaped hole in her world. It feels like he should be here, editorialising for her, giving a running commentary on the mission. Ginny looks across to the typewriter sitting on the dining table, the pile of training manuals from Walden's den she has "borrowed", and she knows they are no real substitute. She's happy, more so than she has been in previous years, but she is beginning to feel like she has gained her happiness at the expense of something she treasured.

The happiness doesn't last, of course; it never could. As June rolls on and the Apollo 11 launch date grows nearer, the press attention becomes more intrusive. The streets of El Lago are thronged with reporters and television vans, and everyone hides indoors for fear of being photographed doing something which might reflect badly on their husbands and NASA. Those stories Ginny heard about the Mercury Seven seem all too plausible, and Ginny isn't even the wife of a "Moonwalker". Yet.

And then she hears rumours from Florida. She knows about the "Cape Cookies", but she foolishly believes it was before Walden's time, or that he at least would stay faithful, she thinks she knows him well enough for that. But there's a story going round about some of the guys and some girls and one of the names Ginny hears is her husband's—someone saw him in a bar with a young woman. The sacrifices Ginny has made, playing the "happy housewife", though she is nothing of the sort, in order not to jeopardise his shot at the Moon. And then he goes and... But did he really? She doesn't want to believe it but she needs to be sure, she can't just ignore it like so many of the other wives do, pretend it's not happening, pretend that it's even okay because he's an astronaut, because he's *a man*.

So Ginny flies to Florida, a commercial flight, hires a car at Orlando Airport, and drives to the Holiday Inn in Cocoa Beach, where the guys stay when they're at the Cape but don't want to stay in astronaut quarters.

She gets out of the rental car and gazes across the parking lot at the entrance to the hotel, and she wonders if she's doing the right thing. Perhaps she should just turn her back on it, ignore it, the way the other wives do. Togethersville has had its casualties over the years, actual deaths, but also those wives who have left their husbands, husbands who have left their wives, like Pam, who left Al in November last year, and Harriet, who divorced Donn. After all those years keeping it together in Togethersville, the cracks are starting to show, and Ginny, who has always felt secure with Walden, she doesn't want her marriage to crash and burn like some others are doing.

Ginny clutches her purse to her bosom and the righteous anger which fuelled her dash across the country, there's nothing left of it, it seems to have vapourised as she drove from the airport, evaporated in the Florida sunshine. She takes her bag from the trunk, and it's a long walk across the lot to the hotel entrance, each step harder to take than the one before, each click of her heels on the asphalt like she's stabbing herself with a knife. And then she reaches the doors and they swoosh apart and she walks into the air-conditioned interior, her footsteps now muffled by carpet.

She had the foresight to book a room before leaving Houston, though she wondered at the time if doing so might tip off her husband. And there he is, standing by the reception desk, clad in his pale blue flight jacket and flight suit, looking bemused, as she approaches. She sees his face

---

"It was upon the waterfront that I first met her, in one of the shabby little tea shops frequented by able sailoresses of the poorer type."
'Friend Island', Francis Stevens (1918)

"Margaret reached over to the other side of the bed where Hank should have been."
'That Only a Mother', Judith Merril (1948)

"What a great day it was for everyone, when David came home from deep space."
'The Woman from Altair', Leigh Brackett (1951)

"Ann Crothers looked at the clock and frowned and turned the fire lower under the bacon."
'Created He Them', Alice Eleanor Jones (1955)

"It was an old house not far from the coast, and had descended generation by generation to the women of the Putnam family."
'The Putnam Tradition', Sonya Dorman (1963)

"Here I am, a silver-haired maiden lady of thirty-five, a feeder of stray cats, a window-ledge gardener, well on my way to the African Violet and antimacassar stage."
'The Warlord of Saturn's Moons', Eleanor Arnason (1974)

"It is impossible to call up the Devil when women are present, I mean real women, that is to say hermaphrodites, for men (real men, who exist) are the people who look at the women, and the women are therefore the people who are looked at by the men."
'Existence', Joanna Russ (1975)

---

and she knows she has done something wrong, but she's not about to admit it, that her sudden dash to Florida might have been prompted by fears Walden has himself a Cape Cookie.

She tells him, I thought it was time to take you up on that offer of a tour of the Cape.

Jeez, Ginny, he says, check with me first.

From his expression, he has a shrewd idea of what has brought her to Cocoa Beach, but is he amused that she might think the worst of him? Should he not be insulted, she thinks—or does that smirk signify he has "cleared everything away" for her arrival? She's over-thinking, she knows she is, life is not a short story, there's no narrative, that's what people *impose* on events in order to make sense of them. But that wide astronaut grin of his, it's starting to annoy Ginny. Her concerns were valid, if only to herself... and perhaps she's reading too much into this, there's no plot, reversal, reveal, resolution, life doesn't work like that. She knows her husband well and she considers herself a good judge of character—she's a writer, after all, and even in science fiction knowing how people work is necessary—but she has to admit she's no wiser now than she was when she left Houston.

We need to talk, says Walden once she has checked in.

He takes her bag and leads her through the lobby and out into the pool area. No peck on the cheek, no hand in the small of her back. She feels his disapproval like something physical has followed them out into the garden. He holds out his hand, she silently places her hotel room key in his palm, he grimaces as he peers at the number and then looks around at the blocks surrounding the garden and pool for her room. Ginny is determined to be unrepentant. She knows NASA is all about the super-family appearance, she has heard stories about the Original Seven and the New Nine, she is an Air Force wife... but if Walden is too dumb, and she has never thought he is, not to realise she has abdicated her life, her wishes and desires to his career, then he's in for a rude awakening.

Once in her room, he puts down her bag and turns to her. I know what goes on, Ginny, he says, but you ought to have more damn faith in me.

They've had their ups and downs, she remembers his moment of foolishness with that fräulein when they were at Ramstein, but she knows Walden is the sort of man who expects no more, and takes no more, than he feels is his due—but he is also a stickler for remaining true to his promises. If she had taken the time to consider it dispassionately, she could guess Walden wouldn't cheat on her. And certainly not with the astronaut groupies who hang around the Cape. And yet...

This is all so new. At Edwards, he was a nobody, now he's in the public eye. Even Ginny has been interviewed on television, been written about in national magazines. She's celebrated. Kind of. For being a wife. Ginny has her fans among the readers of science fiction magazines, but she's still small fry compared to the likes of Catherine, Miriam, Margaret or Zenna. And even new writers like Ursula and Joanna seem to have more impact with their stories than anything Ginny has ever written.

She stands there just inside the door and she has to admit that seeing him in his flight suit—the NASA flight jacket is a bonus—still makes her heart take wing; her flyboy, with his blond hair and his aviator's grin, she never regretted marrying him, even during the years abroad and the years of exile at Edwards. And she moves toward him and if this feels like a bad Hollywood movie, then she's in the mood for bad Hollywood movie sentiments, and reaching him she puts her arms about her husband and pecks him about the mouth and then on the mouth; and he takes charge, as men do, and presses his lips to hers, he reaches up a hand to the back of her head, and the seduction, if that's what it is, Walden is surprisingly ardent, insistent, pushing against what she's willing to let him have, she remembers this from their days courting when she was a student at SDSU but this feels stronger...

Something is unlocked, released, but she never figures out what. They fall onto the bed, feverishly undressing, he strips out of his flight suit, leaving it depending from his booted feet like a pale shadow, she sheds dress, shoes, pantyhose, panties and bra...

Sex: the response to so many marital problems, but so rarely a solution.

The Vehicle Assembly Building is 526 feet tall, so tall in fact, their guide tells Ginny and Walden, that clouds sometimes form inside. It's the largest building in Florida, and the largest single-storey building in the world. Ginny has never visited New York, she has not seen the Empire State Building, the tallest building in the world and nearly three times taller—so she cannot help gawking like a rube as she gazes upward in one of the VAB's empty high bays. She puts a hand on the crown of her hard hat to hold it in place as she cranes her neck, and her eyes travel up endless beams and girders and decks, an Escher-like maze, it's like a forge or a warehouse turned on its end.

A hand grips her arm, and she abruptly returns to earth. The hand belongs to her husband, but the expectant, and amused, gaze on her is their guide's. He gestures for them to follow, and crosses into another of the high bays—but there is something blocking the view and it's only as Ginny enters the bay she sees it's a crawler-transporter tread, and it must be twice her height. The crawler-transporter itself is the size of a large building, like a faculty block from a university campus, and it can *move*.

But then Ginny looks up and she sees white and black, a vast tapering cylinder painted in those colours, stretching up to the roof and seemingly held upright by a tower of red girders. The Saturn V stack is so much bigger than she imagined. She knows it is 363 feet tall, but that's just a number, and like many readers and writers of science fiction she has seen so many numbers so much larger— millions of miles! thousands of years! hundreds of light-years! She has become almost immune to scale, blasé about immensity. But this, it takes her breath away, and she finds it hard to credit three men will be perched atop this rocket and it will carry them to the Moon. She feels humbled, as if the immense physical presence of the crawler-transporter and Saturn V has levered open her imagination and created a gaping void to be filled.

Apollo 12, says the engineer, they finished putting it together only two days ago.

When will it launch? asks Ginny.

There's still weeks of tests yet, the engineer adds. It's all automated, but we won't be ready to roll out to the pad for more than a month.

There is an unintended irony here. I have never visited the John F Kennedy Space Center, nor the Lyndon B Johnson Space Center (as the Manned Spacecraft Center is now known), I have never stood beside a Saturn V. I can only imagine its size, its sheer physicality. And yet, here I am, attempting to describe it in such a way that its overwhelming proportions impact my fictional character's imagination. There are those who consider science fiction an essentially ironic genre, and the universe is indeed indifferent to the plight of humans—but in many science fiction stories, the very fate of the universe is dependent upon a person's actions. In order to tell stories which will appeal to readers, writers must put people at the centre, and give them the power to change their world. It is almost axiomatic.

Yet here is Virginia Grace Eckhardt, who has no such power. She has power only over the fictional worlds she creates on her typewriter. *There* is irony. And there is more irony still—

Imagining an entirely female astronaut corps, given that, at the time Ginny is being shown around the VAB in early July 1969, only one woman, Valentina Tereshkova, has been into space.

Positing a history of science fiction in which the genre is dominated by women, in which it is considered women's fiction.

One of the strengths of science fiction is its capacity to literalise metaphors. The 526 foot tall Vehicle Assembly Building, the Apollo 12 stack on the crawler-transporter in one of its high bays, both could be considered literal representations of the irony which underlies the narrative of *All That Outer Space Allows*.

The view from the roof of the VAB is astonishing, even though there's little to see: low scrub, inlets and basins, to the east the blurred grey carpet of the Atlantic Ocean. And, of course, the two launch pads—a wide causeway stretches from the VAB to each of them, along which the crawler-transporter will carry its Saturn V stack.

A cool sea breeze blows across the top of the VAB, and Ginny feels it press the thin material of her dress against her back. There's a photographer from the NASA press office standing several feet away, so Ginny smiles and grips Walden's hand tighter and hopes she doesn't look too foolish in the hard hat. The photographer tells them he's finished, Walden releases her hand and marches across to have a word with the man. Ginny turns about, puts a hand up to the NASA pass clipped to her dress and plays idly with it as she gazes out at launch pads 39A and 39B. At some point in the next year or two, her husband may well find himself lying on his back in a command module atop 6 million pounds of fuel—kerosene and liquid oxygen; and liquid hydrogen and liquid oxygen—which will burn producing 8.5 million pounds of thrust and all to throw around 45 tons into orbit about the Earth in eleven and a half minutes.

She wonders what it might feel like to sit atop a Saturn V mated to one of those giant red gantries at the launch pad, clad in a space suit, the battleship grey instrument panel above her... She hugs her torso and shivers. This is what she has been writing about, but now having witnessed the colossal size of the Saturn V, she wonders if she can truly capture the sensation of flying in it. Science fiction seems such an imperfect tool, too dependent upon well-worn tropes and conventions so long established they're usually left unexplained.

If only Ginny could apply to be an astronaut herself! But women are not allowed. Women are perfectly capable of being astronauts, of that much she is convinced—and an all-female astronaut corps would do the job just as well as an all-male one, if not better. Perhaps there's a story in there somewhere, a history of the US space program, but with female astronauts—

Walden is at her side. He'll send us copies, he says. Have you seen enough, hon?

She glances at her watch. It's after four, they've been here since lunch-time, no doubt the tour would not have taken so long if Ginny hadn't insisted on asking their guide how everything worked. He seemed as fascinated by her interest as she was by his explanations.

What about the launch pads? she asks. Can we see one of those?

Not with the Apollo 11 stack on the pad, hon, maybe another time.

Walden insinuates an arm around her waist. I got to get back to work, he says. Tomorrow maybe I'll take you round the MSOB. I can show you the altitude chambers.

He gives her a squeeze and steers her about, toward the stairwell in the centre of the roof. I'll come to the hotel this evening, he adds, we can have dinner in the restaurant. Another squeeze. Maybe I'll even stay over.

I'd like that, she replies.

In the VAB parking lot, no longer wearing hard hats, Ginny glances back at the building and is struck anew by its enormous size. Science fiction is all about scale, vast distances and deep time, made manageable, made *human*. All those parsecs and light years, those millions and billions of years, rendered *conceivable*. And yet real space exploration is huge too, perhaps just a little bit too large to be believed, even when standing right next to it. The Saturn V seen up close is... *monstrous*.

And the distances! How obliviously science fiction skates over the vastness of space—*a quarter of a million miles* to the Moon, three days travel, they say the guys in Apollo 10 travelled the fastest of any human beings, hitting 24,791 mph during their return from the Moon. And a trip to Mars... It almost doesn't bear thinking about: millions of miles, months and months of travel, to stand on the surface of a world where a man cannot survive without science, without engineering... *This* is what Ginny wants to put into her science fiction.

She has stood on the flight line at Edwards, she has seen Boeing B-52 Stratofortress bombers and marvelled at their size, been astonished that such a large and substantial aircraft—length 159 feet 4 inches, wingspan 185 feet, max takeoff weight 488,000 lbs!—could ever take to the air. But she has seen them fly, thundering past, no more than a few hundred feet above the dry lake, trailing smoke, the roar of their eight turbofan engines deafening.

Ginny knows about sense of wonder and suspension of disbelief, they are the tools of her trade. She tries to deploy both in her stories, whether she succeeds is open to debate. Sometimes she speculates if applying those concepts to real life, the quotidian and the prosaic, in some way devalues them. After all, she has witnessed much which would seem to apply—not just the sight of a B-52 taking off, but the ways of men, of her husband, the selective blindness and pigheadedness. The efforts she must go to in order to be noticed, the work she must put into the house so it fits Walden's idea of a home...

Ginny slides into Walden's car, and as soon as she's shut the door, he pulls out of the parking space. I'll take you back to your car, he says, I still got stuff to do.

But you'll come to the hotel later?

Sure, I said so, didn't I? He looks across at her. How long are you planning on staying, hon?

She ignores his gaze and stares out of the passenger window at the passing scenery, which appears no more interesting at ground level than it did 526 feet up in the air. I don't know, she replies. A couple of days, I suppose.

When you've seen everything at the Cape, there's the beach, Walden suggests.

Ginny is not a beach person, and spending hours lying on hot sand beneath the Florida sun, in a bikini or a one-piece, that's not something she's ever considered a worthwhile pastime. She came to Cocoa Beach to see more of the space program—and her husband of course—not to sunbathe.

Maybe, Ginny tells her husband.

Walden Eckhardt

From Wikipedia, the free encyclopedia

Walden Jefferson "Wal" Eckhardt (born March 8, 1932) is a retired United States Air Force brigadier general and a former NASA astronaut. As the lunar module pilot for Apollo 15 in 1971, he became the eighth person to walk on the Moon.

Biography

Early life and education
Eckhardt was born in Grand Junction, Colorado, where he graduated from Central High School in 1950. After a year spent working at Walker Field Airport, where he earned his pilot's licence, he studied for and received a Bachelor of Science in Aeronautical Engineering at San Diego State University in 1955.

Military career
Eckhardt joined the United States Air Force on graduation from San Diego State University. After a year at flying school, he was sent to George Air Force Base, California, for advanced training on the North American F-86 Sabre fighter jet, before being assigned in 1959 to the 415th Interceptor Squadron stationed at Ramstein Air Force Base in Germany. In 1962, he was transferred to the Experimental Test Pilot School at Edwards Air Force Base, California. On graduation, he remained at Edwards as an instructor before attending the Aerospace Research Pilot School in 1962. After graduating from ARPS, he spent a year as an instructor and was then assigned to the Fighter Test Group.

NASA career
In April 1966, Eckhardt was one of the nineteen selected for NASA's fifth group of astronauts. In 1968, he served as a member of the support crew for Apollo 10, the first mission to carry the full Apollo stack to the Moon and the dry run for the first manned Moon landing. He then served as backup lunar module pilot for Apollo 12, the second Moon landing mission, commanded by Charles 'Pete' Conrad.

Apollo 15
Between July 26 and August 7, 1971 – as the Apollo 15 Lunar Module Pilot (LMP) – Eckhardt logged 295 hours and 11 minutes in space. His extra-vehicular activity (EVA) on the Moon's surface

amounted to 18 hours and 35 minutes of the mission time (an additional 33 minutes was used to do a stand-up EVA by opening the LM's docking hatch to survey the surroundings and take photographs). Eckhardt and David Scott's mission was more science-based than previous missions, which meant that they received intensive geological training to meet the demanding nature of the J-Mission profile. This extra training is credited with allowing them to make one of the most important discoveries of the Apollo era, the Genesis Rock.

Apollo 15 landed in the Moon's Hadley-Apennine region, noted for its mountains and rilles. As a J-Mission, they would spend more time on the moon than previous missions, to allow for three EVAs. As well, Eckhardt was the first automobile passenger on the Moon as Scott drove the Lunar Roving Vehicle (LRV) carried along for this mission in the Lunar Module (LM) Falcon's Descent Stage. Scott and Eckhardt's stay on the Moon was just under three days at 66 hours and 54 minutes.

Post-NASA career
After Apollo 15, Eckhardt remained with NASA after being assigned to the Skylab program. However, once the planned fifth Skylab mission was cancelled Eckhardt left NASA, and retired from the United States Air Force, on September 1, 1975. He held a number of positions with aerospace companies before retiring in 1992.

Personal life
Eckhardt married his wife, Virginia, shortly after she graduated from San Diego State University in 1958. They have one daughter, Suzy, born 1973. The pair divorced in 1979.

Organizations

He was a member of the Air Force Association and the Society of Experimental Test Pilots.

Awards and Honors

- Air Force Distinguished Service Medal
- Air Force Commendation Medal
- NASA Distinguished Service Medal
- Command Pilot Astronaut Wings
- Robert J Collier Trophy, 1971
- Haley Astronautics Award, 1972

He was also awarded Belgium's Order of Leopold in 1971, and an Honorary Doctorate in Aeronautical Engineering from San Diego State University in 1971.

He was inducted into the International Space Hall of Fame in 1983, and the U.S. Astronaut Hall of Fame on October 4, 1997.

Bibliography

- *Flight of the Falcon* (with Virginia G. Eckhardt, 1983)

Chapter 9
Lunar Module Descent

The next day, Ginny is taken round the Manned Spacecraft Operations Building, she sees the altitude chambers in which they test if the command modules and lunar modules can survive the rigours of space. She can't decide if the chambers resemble giant ovens or giant diving bells but perhaps, she decides, it's because their function is something of both. Then, on the third floor, Walden hasn't said where he's taking her, he abruptly halts, glances at his watch and swears.

I was supposed to be somewhere, he says, I got to make a phone call. Wait here, I'll be back in a minute, hon.

He hurries off back toward the elevators, leaving Ginny on her own in the corridor, wondering if she's meant to stand there like a lemon until he returns. And then the doors just a little further along the corridor swing open and a woman with short brown hair, dressed in a white nurse's uniform and white hose, comes striding toward Ginny, and frowns on seeing her and asks, Can I help you?

Ginny introduces herself but is only halfway through explaining her husband is giving her a tour of the MSOB but has just abandoned her to make a telephone call, when the nurse interrupts, and with a smile asks, He was taking you to the suiting room?

I guess, says Ginny.

Well, it's this way, come on, I'll take you. My name is Dee, by the way.

She leads Ginny along the corridor and through a pair of double doors into a white-walled room with several tan Naugahyde armchairs scattered about it. Each armchair faces a large white control-panel festooned with dials and valves and knobs; and between each control panel, a waist-high table stretches from the wall out into the room. Dee waves at a man in white coveralls, he's standing at one of the tables and Ginny thinks he's talking to someone lying on the table top before she realises it's an empty spacesuit.

Apollo A7L Materials
(See Figure 5.25)

Layer*	Material	Function
	Extravehicular (EV) Suit	
	(rear entry zipper)	
1	Teflon cloth	Abrasion/flame resistance
2	Beta cloth (Teflon-coated silica fiber)	Fire protection (non-flammable in oxygen atmosphere)
3,5	Aluminized griddle Kapton	Reflective insulation
4,6	Beta marquisette (Teflon-coated silica fiber, laminated to Kapton)	Spacer between reflective surfaces
7,9,11,13,15	Aluminized Mylar	Reflective insulation
8,10,12,14	Nonwoven Dacron	Spacer
16	Neoprene-coated nylon	Inner liner
17	Nylon	Restraint layer for pressurized bladder
18	Neoprene-coated nylon	Bladder material serving as an impermeable layer containing suit-pressurization oxygen
19	Neoprene convolute	Pressure-retaining flexible joints
20	Knit jersey laminate	Abrasion protection
21	Lightweight Nomex cloth	Comfort
	Liquid Cooling Garment (LCG)	
22	Nylon spandex	Holds tubing close to skin
23	Vinyl tubing	Water distribution for cooling
24	Porous lightweight nylon	Comfort
	Intravehicular (IV) Suit	
1	Teflon-coated Beta cloth	Fire protection (non-flammable in oxygen atmosphere)
2	Nomex cloth	Snag/fire protection
3	Nylon	Restraint layer for pressurized bladder
4	Neoprene-coated nylon	Bladder material serving as an impermeable layer containing suit-pressurization oxygen
5	Lightweight Nomex cloth	Comfort
	Constant Wear Garment (CWG)	
1	Cotton	Comfort

*Materials are listed from outside to inside

Hey, Joe, says Dee, this is Ginny, you want to give her a quick run-down of what you do in here?

Ginny Eckhardt, Ginny adds, Walden just had to go make

a phone call.

She looks at the spacesuit on the table, and asks, Is that what they'll be wearing on the Moon?

Joe starts to explain the A7L and its twenty-one layers of materials, from the rubber-coated nylon bladder to the Teflon fabric abrasion layer. When he mentions the spacesuits are made by a division of Playtex, Ginny can't help smiling—and she thinks about bras and foundation garments, girdles and corsets, and the white constricting material from which they're made, the outer layer of the A7L shares their colour and texture. And the A7L's innermost layer of nylon too, she's amused by these manliest of men wearing garments so closely related to women's underwear. Joe is in the middle of an explanation of the connectors on the front of the torso, and Ginny is listening fascinated, when the doors to the suiting room swing open and Ginny turns and sees Walden poke his head inside, scan the room, scowl, and then withdraw. She makes a face at Dee, puzzled by her husband's behaviour; but then she turns back to Joe and he has what looks like a fishbowl in his hands and he tells her it's the helmet and it's made of polycarbonate...

Joe drifts away after his lecture, and Ginny and Dee chat. They connect immediately, it's not simply their shared gender in this predominantly male world, or the fact they're the same age, perhaps it's the interest Ginny showed in the A7L, in what it takes to put a man on the Moon. For Ginny, it's partly gratitude at being rescued in the corridor, the chances of someone she knows passing were slim, and she thinks perhaps there are not many at the Cape who would have stopped to ask if she needed help. Emboldened by Dee's friendliness, Ginny admits she writes science fiction, and Dee mentions a writer who interviewed her years before as research for a novel about a space nurse.

That novel is *Countdown for Cindy* by Eloise Engle, originally published in 1962 in the magazine *American Girl*. I own a copy of the 1964 Bantam paperback. It is the sort of science fiction novel which proves the point of Ginny. In the novel, Cindy, the protagonist, is celebrated by a shocked and astounded media as the first woman into space when she is chosen to accompany a doctor of space medicine to the US Moon base. The book was written, of course, before Tereshkova's flight aboard Vostok 6. *Countdown for Cindy* is rife with late fifties gender politics— these are not the sensibilities Ginny, who is fictional herself, would write into her own stories, although she has lived with them and not much has changed for the better in the decade since.

There is a scene in Engle's novel which, for me, is emblematic of the time's attitudes to women—shortly after arriving at the Moon base, Cindy gets ready for her first shift on duty: "Then she opened her bag and took out fresh disposable undies and a pair of clean slacks. She thought a moment. What a horrid mistake that would be. She folded the slacks, put them away, and took out her crisp white nurse's uniform and the perky cap. Yes, that was more like it. White hose and white shoes... she looked into the mirror and applied fresh lipstick on her lips. Ready? Not quite. A bit of perfume and a final smoothing of her fluffy hair". Cindy is expected to *look* like a nurse, no matter how impractical her uniform in one-sixth gravity; and she must look pretty too.

Ten minutes later, Walden sticks his head back into the suiting room, he spots Dee and says, Have you seen my wife— Oh there you are, Ginny.

Before they go, Ginny needs to visit a rest-room, Walden of course has no idea where one for women can be found, but Dee gives precise directions. After washing her hands and fixing her lipstick, Ginny returns to her husband, and she says her goodbyes to Dee, with promises to keep in touch; and then Walden walks Ginny to the elevator, they descend to the first floor, leave the building and he drives her to the visitor center parking lot, where she left her rental. Walden tells her he'll be round to see her that evening and they'll go out for dinner, and she wonders if she has brought enough clothes to eat out every night of her stay in Florida. She gets in her car, winds down the window, they kiss through it, and Walden turns on his heel and strides back to his car, while she inserts her ignition key and gives it a thoughtful twist.

It has been like a holiday these days at the Cape. Each evening, he takes her somewhere different to eat—Ramon's Restaurant, The Moon Hut, Fat Boys Bar-B-Q Restaurant, Bernard's Surf, Wolfie's Restaurant... And everywhere they go, they know Walden, they know he's one of the Apollo astronauts and they tell him he's going to the Moon for sure. She can see why he frequents these places, it's not just for the food. Ginny loves the history, the space memorabilia on display—there are wooden plaques naming the Mercury Seven astronauts on the walls of Ramon's, signed photographs and "flown items" in the other venues.

And having Walden in her bed every night, it's doing both of them good, the sex is better than it has been for a long time. Walden is more relaxed, he flashes that aviator grin of his more often; Ginny feels wanted, no longer an accessory, but a *partner*. They talk, and it's silly stuff, trivial chatter, they laugh and joke, they have fun together. Walden, for the first time, tells her a little bit about what he's doing, and he's surprised and delighted when she understands some of it.

Remember when I showed you the LM simulator, he says, I thought you were going to fly the damn thing all the way to the Moon.

I wish I could, she says wistfully.

They're lying in bed, only just covered by rumpled sheets, the lights are off and the room glows with moonlight the same colour as the polished skin of a command module. Ginny smiles indulgently. She rolls onto her side, facing Walden, and props her head on her palm. He is gazing up at the ceiling and he's talking but she's not

120

taking in the words. She spent today on the beach, basking beneath the sun, and she can feel the heat she took in radiating from her, she is golden with it, and she doesn't feel like a member of the Astronaut Wives Club for the first time since moving to Houston, she feels like a *wife*. Grateful, she bends forward and pecks her husband on the lips, silencing him.

The "couple of days" turns into a week. Ginny has seen all there is to see at the Cape, but she is enjoying her husband's company too much to want to return to the empty house in El Lago. She explores the surrounding area but there is little of interest, people come here for the beach and the astronauts. She finds a small book store with a reasonable science fiction selection, buys a couple of new paperbacks— one by Kate and one by Marion—and reads them as she lays on the beach, for the first time in her life finding pleasure in pure indolence, enjoying the way the heat soaks into her body, causing her to gently and effortlessly perspire, and, though she would never admit it, she is even gratified by the speculative looks she receives from passing men.

But it has to end, she's known since the first night it would end, she can't stay here forever. Walden tells her over drinks in the Riviera Lounge:

The other guys, he says, they don't like it if the wives stay too long. You have Houston, we have the Cape. You put us off our training.

But I'm interested in all this, she protests.

Yeah, you see, he says, that's what wrong. I mean, I never said anything about your stories, about your women's magazines, with their spaceships and robots. I mean, hell, it's all make-believe, right?

He adopts the serious face he likes to use when he's about to tell her something he thinks she doesn't know but is secretly afraid she already does. She has never had the heart to tell him he is usually right to be scared—but marriages survive on the discretion of wives.

You're like a distraction, Walden tells her; you *are* a distraction. I have to give it one hundred percent, I can't have anything around that affects my focus.

You have to go back to Houston, he says.

She's been feeling a need to write, prompted by the two novels she's just read, and by what she's learnt here at the Cape, so she's sort of glad the idyll is over. But it still hurts to be told to go away by her husband.

He reaches across the table, takes her hand and squeezes. It's been real good, Ginny, he says, having you here, but the holiday is over.

She gives a wan smile, picks up her piña colada and sucks on the straw, but then her eyes narrow as something occurs to her. What about the Apollo 11 launch, she asks, can I stay for that?

In just over a week, Neil Armstrong, Buzz Aldrin and Mike Collins will be heading for the Moon, and four days later they will make the first lunar landing, they will be the first people to set foot on an alien world in the history of humankind.

I think you should go home, Walden says firmly.

Ginny really wants to see the Apollo 11 liftoff, and not on television. But she will not plead, she will not wheedle. There will be other launches. And she *is* missing her Hermes Baby. Her head is full of ideas, baked to a lustrous finish beneath the sun during her hours on the beach, she has written stories in her head as she sunbathed, has dreamt up plots, narratives, settings, and she wants to get them down on paper before she loses them forever.

I'll book a flight tomorrow, she says.

Walden's mood abruptly improves, and he grins and lifts his own scotch and branch water and salutes Ginny.

And she thinks, if only *she* were so easy to please, if only spousal obedience were enough to make *her* happy—but Ginny ordering Walden about is almost unthinkable, although there are science fiction stories where women

122

dominate: Francis Stevens even wrote one back in 1918! For now, however, Ginny will have to settle for her husband's faithfulness.

And she knows she's richer than many of the other astronaut wives for having it.

Ginny's impromptu holiday has had a salutary effect on her. Back in El Lago, she spends a day cleaning the house from top to bottom, getting down on her hands and knees to scrub the kitchen floor, polishing the faucets in the bathrooms until they shine like the skin of a LM, taking the rugs out into the yard and beating them until her arm aches. She rearranges the kitchen cupboards, emptying them, wiping down the shelves, and then deciding what will now go where. Walden can never find anything, so it doesn't matter if everything has moved.

Only when Ginny is satisfied the house is as clean as it will ever be—and she marvels at the pride she is taking in her home, and she thinks of the years at Edwards and the dust that covered everything and how some things, *most* things, seemed more important than whether the house was neat and tidy and clean... It's not just her home however, now she even spends time fussing over her appearance, each morning powdering her face and painting her lips, mascara and eyeshadow, plucking her eyebrows, styling her hair, doing it *every day*; she wears nice dresses, heels that match, keeps her nails shaped and polished... She is well-groomed, and she takes satisfaction in being so.

Ginny's flying visit to the Cape was also a holiday from Ginny the astronaut wife. That healthy glow she sees in the mirror each morning is not just suntan. But now she is back home, and she has to think about the house and she has to always look presentable, and her head is brimming with ideas for stories she wants to write. For the first time in such a long time, deep in her heart she knows that Mrs Walden J Eckhardt and Virginia G Parker are one and the same person. So she makes herself a jug of iced tea, and she fetches the Hermes Baby and a sheaf of paper from the closet, and still in the white balloon-sleeved blouse and black skirt and waistcoat combination she dressed in that morning she goes to the dining table. She does not need her slacks, she does not need her plaid shirt. (But she does slip off her peep-toe heels.)

When Ginny was in the MSOB being shown one of the altitude chambers, a great steel drum of a room, with thick hatches and small portholes, like something you'd expect to find in the deepest abyss of the ocean... Peering into the altitude chamber, it occurred to Ginny the surface of Mars is no less inimical than the surface of the Moon. She's read all those stories by Leigh and Catherine, the ones where Mars resembles the Mojave Desert more than the actual Red Planet, but Ginny has an idea for a story about the first mission to a realistic Mars, and she wonders if it is possible to make the journey using the same technology as the Apollo program. But three men—or in her story, women—cooped up in such a tiny space for a week is plausible, it's what happened on Apollo 8 and 10... But for months? Perhaps even a year or more? She wonders if there are designs for bigger spacecraft on the drawing board somewhere—after all, what is NASA going to do once the Moon flights are over? Mars is the next obvious target.

She doesn't know enough about the science. Walden's manuals, the ones that are not general spaceflight texts, are exclusively about the Apollo spacecraft and flights to the Moon. Maybe some sort of space station could be used—it doesn't have to be large, just big enough for two astronauts and their supplies on a trip of two years or so to Mars and back...

And what would they find there? She needs some sort of twist... And her thoughts spiral back to Catherine and Leigh and their stories and she thinks: ruins! Her Mars astronauts will find ancient alien ruins; and in among them they will discover something which changes the history of

124

humankind, something which... gives humanity the stars. Yes, she likes that idea. Her astronauts find plans for a space drive invented by aliens, who visited Earth and Mars billions of years before...

Ginny tucks one foot under herself and begins typing. She leaves the title blank for now; later, as the story develops, perhaps something suitable will occur to her...

Reporters prowl the streets of El Lago and Nassau Bay; television trucks line the roads. Ginny peers through a gap in the curtains as cars, men in suits, women in smart jackets and skirts, bearing a bewildering array of network logos, pass by. They're not there for her, but Jan, Joan and Pat. Ginny doesn't know the three women well, they're New Nine and the Fourteen, and while she's met them at the AWC and Jan at the Scotts', Ginny has remained on the outer edges of Togethersville. Having no children has proven not just a lack of common ground but also a barrier between herself and the other wives. Nor does Ginny go to church, or involve herself in community theatre or local schools. Ginny's private life, her secret career, is not one she can share with Togethersville.

Early on the morning of 16 July, Ginny sits down to watch the Apollo 11 launch on her own, wishing she were at the Cape to witness the liftoff in person. Afterward, she telephones Mary, Ginny feels she can talk to her since both Joe and Walden were on the support crew for Apollo 10 and Joe is backup LMP on Apollo 14, which means he will fly on Apollo 17, two missions after Walden. Walden and Joe will one day ride a Saturn V into orbit, so Ginny and Mary want Apollo 11 to succeed—and are secretly hoping it might fail.

Not fail *catastrophically*—Ginny doesn't think she could handle it if Neil, Buzz and Mike were killed; and she has no desire to wish such a fate upon them, or their families.

I heard, says Ginny, the lunar surface might be like a sea of dust and the LM will just sink into it.

Oh no, breathes Mary, you think so?

They've sent probes to the Moon, haven't they? I don't think they sank.

What do you think will happen?

Exactly what everyone expects, Ginny reassures her. They know what they're doing, they've been training for this for years.

It's kind of fun playing what-if, but it's unfair to inflict it on Mary, who is an astronaut wife and not one of Ginny's friends from science fiction.

And speaking of "what-ifs", Ginny does not know it, but the following year, Joe Engle is replaced on Apollo 17 by Jack Schmitt, who was assigned as LMP on Apollo 18. Budget cuts resulted in the cancellation of Apollo 18 in September 1970, and the scientific community lobbied for geologist Schmitt to replace test pilot Engle on Apollo 17. Engle, who already had his astronaut wings from the X-15 program, later went on to fly in the Space Shuttle program.

But it's safe, asks Mary, isn't it?

Everything has been tested hundreds, thousands, of times, Ginny says, Nothing will fail.

This is not to say the astronaut wives are not worried about Apollo 11, although they seem to have plenty of faith in the equipment—as recorded in *First on the Moon*, the first official account of Apollo 11, "written by" Armstrong, Aldrin and Collins, with the assistance of *Time* journalists Gene Farmer and Dora Jane Hamblin: "In El Lago Jan Armstrong was ticking off the minutes, but not out of any particular safety concern; her concern was still the one she had expressed much earlier; would they be able to do all they had been assigned to do on this first lunar landing mission?"

The images on the television are blurred and ghostly, Ginny leans forward, not entirely sure what she's seeing. There's a dim white figure, with a bulbous head and a large pack on its back, descending a dark shape on the left, and then the figure drops the last couple of feet, and Neil's voice, distorted from its 250,000-mile journey as radio waves, says, That's one small step for man, one giant leap for mankind.

And Ginny thinks, what? That doesn't make sense—

But the announcer is now saying Neil actually said, one small step for *a* man; and Ginny laughs and salutes the television with her cup of coffee. She wonders how long it took Neil to think up those words—she knows they're going to be remembered, they have that quality which suggests

```
109:24:23 Armstrong: That's one small step for (a)
man; one giant leap for mankind. (Long Pause)

109:24:48 Armstrong: Yes, the surface is fine and
powdery. I can kick it up loosely with my toe. It
does adhere in fine layers, like powdered charcoal,
to the sole and sides of my boots. I only go in a
small fraction of an inch, maybe an eighth of an
inch, but I can see the footprints of my boots and
the treads in the fine, sandy particles.

109:25:30 McCandless: Neil, this is Houston. We're
copying. (Long Pause)

109:25:46 Armstrong: Ah ... There seems to be no
difficulty in moving around - as we suspected. It's
even perhaps easier than the simulations of one-
sixth g that we performed in the various
simulations on the ground. It's absolutely no
trouble to walk around. (Pause)

109:26:16 Armstrong: Okay. The descent engine did
not leave a crater of any size. It has about 1 foot
clearance on the ground. We're essentially on a
very level place here. I can see some evidence of
rays emanating from the descent engine, but a very
insignificant amount. (Pause)

109:26:54 Armstrong: Okay, Buzz, we ready to bring
down the (70 mm Hasselblad) camera?
```

they'll echo down the ages, just like the first lines of some novels, "It is a truth universally acknowledged, that a single man in possession of a good fortune, must be in want of a wife", or "You will rejoice to hear that no disaster has accompanied the commencement of an enterprise which you have regarded with such evil forebodings".

And now Neil in his spacesuit is bouncing up and down, as if he were filled with some gas lighter than air, although, of course, there is no air on the Moon; but Ginny thinks it must be exhilarating to have such freedom of movement, even if neither Neil nor Buzz can actually *touch* their surroundings, sealed as they are inside layers of rubber, kevlar, mylar, Beta-cloth and whatever other materials are involved. And Ginny even bounces up and down herself on the sofa, almost spilling her coffee, and then she laughs and swears at herself for being so childish. But it looks like so much *fun*, Neil and Buzz jumping around on the lunar surface, it's something she has never considered in all her imaginings about the Moon landing—although, now she thinks about it, she bets it's hard work inside those suits, she remembers the one Joe showed her at the Cape, those thick gauntlets, how difficult it must be to even bend your fingers, how hard to lift an arm, bend a knee, even in one-sixth gravity.

Like millions of other people scattered around the world, Ginny sits entranced by the poor quality television pictures being broadcast from the lunar surface. She thinks about her own unsuccessful attempts at a story describing a lunar mission and it occurs to her it's more than just the spacecraft. Simply presenting spaceflight in a realistic manner is not enough—she has to get across to the reader what it actually *feels* like, she must write in such a way a reader can truly understand and empathise with her protagonist. The Apollo program is a wonderful adventure, an amazing endeavour, and it seems to Ginny it would be a shame for science fiction to ignore it.

—☽—

Chapter 10
"We have touchdown"

Apollo 12 in December is almost an anticlimax—these missions could never be commonplace, but so much was invested in Apollo 11, in being *first*, anything which followed was sure to be seen in a lesser light. What an astonishing thing NASA has done, will the human race ever again accomplish anything so marvellous: *to set foot on an alien world*. Twice to date, and more to come. In these times of Mutually Assured Destruction, Soviet aircraft encroaching on US and NATO airspace, USAF interceptors hurtling into clear blue skies on a regular basis... Some days it seems to Ginny humanity has reached its pinnacle.

But before that happens, NASA has more to do, and in late March 1970, it announces the crew for Apollo 15, so now it's official: Walden is going to the Moon. Ginny's stock in the AWC has been slowly rising since late 1969 when the Apollo 15 crew started training, but now it's out in the open and the pressure is on. When she considers what some of the other wives have been going through, Ginny realises she is lucky. She and Walden go well together, she reached an accommodation with the danger inherent in his job years ago, and though what he's now doing is so much more dangerous, she has faith, perhaps even more than Walden does, in the hardware and the engineering. Of course, they have it better than most—no kids; and if Ginny has never quite plugged into Togethersville, she still has her friends in science fiction scattered across the country, she still has her writing. She made a conscious decision to support Walden when he joined NASA, and she has stuck to that, and she has been very fortunate nothing has happened to distract her from it.

Which is more than be said for real astronaut Jim Irwin, whose wife Mary was beset by tragedy, and consequently their marriage was slowly disintegrating, while he was

---

APOLLO 15 LAUNCH JULY 26

The 12-day Apollo 15 mission, scheduled for launch on July 26 to carry out the fourth United States manned exploration of the Moon will:
- Double the time and extend tenfold the range of lunar surface exploration as compared with earlier missions;
- Deploy the third in a network of automatic scientific stations;
- Conduct a new group of experiments in lunar orbit; and
- Return to Earth a variety of lunar rock and soil samples.
Scientists expect the results will greatly increase man's knowledge of both the Moon's history and composition and of the evolution and dynamic interaction of the Sun-Earth system.
This is so because the dry, airless, lifeless Moon still bears records of solar radiation and the early years of solar system history that have been erased from Earth. Observations of current lunar events also may increase understanding of similar processes on Earth, such as earthquakes.
The Apollo 15 lunar module will make its descent over the Apennine peaks, one of the highest mountain ranges on the Moon, to land near the rim of the canyon-like Hadley Rille. From this Hadley-Apennine lunar base, between the mountain range and the rille, Commander David R. Scott and Lunar Module Pilot Walden J. Eckhardt will explore several kilometers from the lunar module, driving an electric-powered lunar roving vehicle for the first time on the Moon.

---

training for Apollo 15. He writes in his autobiography, *To Rule the Night*: "I thought the woman should be there to assist the man, help him in his task".

Irwin's attitude was hardly unique among astronauts, or

indeed men in general—either in the real world, or the fictional world of *All That Outer Space Allows*. If Ginny is happy to give the impression she is thoroughly committed to supporting her man, and if she feels her reward for doing so—being a part of the space program, even if only peripherally—is perhaps not enough, that she doesn't have the best of the bargain, and even their new-found affluence, and the fame too, is no real prize either, she keeps silent for Walden's sake. Ginny would like to be known as a science fiction writer, not an astronaut wife; and the two forms of celebrity simply do not compare. When she finishes her toilet each morning and inspects her made up features, and she thinks of all she once held dear and has now compromised, the real Ginny Eckhardt hidden beneath all those Revlon products crowding the top of her dressing-table; and she sometimes wishes she could throw it all away and go back to who *she* wants to be, not who NASA and the AWC and Walden want her to be, to who she *was*... Except, of course, she never was that woman, the Ginny of Edwards is no less fictional than the Ginny she presents to people in Houston, a consequence of misremembering, confabulation, nostalgia and wish-fulfilment.

Ginny tries hard not to let her new status change her, and she finds the increased press attention a little embarrassing—perhaps she's afraid some enterprising reporter might dig up her science fiction stories, and it would be horrible if that prevented Walden from going to the Moon... Although she has had nothing published since 'The Spaceships Men Don't See' and that was just over two years ago. In her more reflective moments, Ginny is worried she is now incapable of writing sellable stories, that the new Ginny of Houston, Texas, is too much the astronaut wife, too much the *wife*, and not enough Virginia G Parker. But these new stories she's working on, the ones editors don't seem to want, she thinks they're worth the effort she's putting into them, she's convinced soon something will break and Cele or Bea or Fanny or Evelyn will send her a contract by return post. So, while Walden is off at the Cape, or Long Island, or wherever the hell he is this week, and the house is empty, the house is clean and tidy, Ginny is dressed and made up, should anyone drop by, during those moments of free time she works on her stories, revises and restructures the rejected ones, types out first drafts of new ones. She keeps on writing, even if she has nothing to say, it's old advice but it works damn it, and better 3,000 words, and "THE END", to be worked on and rewritten, than half a page that goes nowhere.

April 1970 and Apollo 13 puts the space program back on the front page, but not for the right reasons. Halfway to the Moon, an oxygen tank in the service module explodes and suddenly the crew of three, Jim Lovell, Fred Haise and Jack Swigert, could die in space. Once again, the streets are mobbed with reporters, and they're at their thickest around the houses of Marilyn and Mary (Jack is one of the program's few bachelors). Togethersville swings into action, and even Ginny finds herself running groceries into the besieged Lovell home in Timber Cove; and she does her best to sympathise with Marilyn, but like all the astronaut wives she's privately glad it's not Walden up there.

But NASA shows what it's made of, and they get the guys home safely, the command module splashes down in the South Pacific, southwest of Samoa and only four miles from the recovery ship.

In September of that year, the dream dies a little when Apollo 18 through 20 are cancelled, and even the promise of a space station, Skylab, can't lessen the hurt. Some of the rookies who were down for those cancelled missions, they're angry and disappointed, and Ginny hears it from their wives. It's worse for the scientists, who are especially bitter that Apollo will forever remain the preserve of test pilots and fighter pilots. Man should go to the Moon for science, NASA should send scientists, but that's not going to happen now.

So Walden and Dave have to learn the science if the scientists are going to get any useful data out of the mission, and that means trip after trip to Hawaii, the San Gabriel Mountains, the Coso Hills, even back to the Mojave Desert, to learn geology. When Walden is home on his infrequent stay overs, he complains he's a pilot not a rock hunter, but as the weeks and months pass his attitude changes and he surprises Ginny by getting excited as he talks geology. He's learnt something new, something completely outside the world in which he has lived his entire life, and the wonder of it animates him whenever he discusses it. Now he wants to go to the Moon not because it's there, not because it will put him at the top of the pyramid, not because putting a man on the lunar surface is such a bold enterprise... No, he wants to go because he might find some *really exciting* rocks on the Moon.

By the end of January 1971, when Apollo 14 launches, Togethersville is undergoing changes. There have been two intakes of astronauts since Walden and Ginny arrived, but plenty of people have also left, and that sense of community, the one Ginny never quite plugged into, it's slowly fading away. Only Al, who is commanding Apollo 14, and Deke, who has never flown, remain from the Original Seven. Neil is retiring and Frank has left from the Next Nine; of the Fourteen, Buzz and Wally Cunningham are going, and Mike has already gone. No one from the Original Nineteen, Walden's group, has spoken of leaving NASA, but with so many astronauts, so few flights and so much uncertainty about what comes next, Ginny thinks more will go in the next couple of years. In fact, what will she and Walden do after he's flown on Apollo 15? It's scheduled for that summer—will he want to stay in the astronaut corps, or return to USAF? It's no good asking him, she drops a few hints on the infrequent weekends he's home, but he doesn't know how to answer. His head is full of Apollo and geology, and he's so tightly focused on his mission he can't even conceive of a world after it.

Ginny is having her own problems imagining a world for her stories. Perhaps that's why she's having so little success selling them, the world in which they're set is the real world, more or less. It's not the Mars of Northwest Smith, nor Ursula's Ekumen. Take this one she's currently working on, about a flight to the Moon which turns into disaster when the spacecraft runs out of fuel and in a decaying orbit. It's an Apollo spacecraft—the astronauts aboard it are on their way to a Moon base, although she suspects there will never be a Moon base, the cancellation of all the flights after Apollo 17 has seen to that. But who knows what the future will bring? Despite this, she has set her story in 1985. Fifteen years into the future. Perhaps space flight will be routine by then—or rather, more routine than the press seems to be treating Apollo 14.

After nearly five years in Houston as an astronaut wife—the AWC meetings for coffee and cake at the Lakewood Yacht Club ended before Apollo 11 launched—but Louise Shepard is someone Ginny barely knows at all. She's an Original Seven wife, and a Boston Brahmin, and she moves in completely different circles. The Shepards don't even live in Nassau Bay, El Lago or Timber Cove, but in River Oaks. Al Shepard, a man Walden respects but does not like, is going to walk on the Moon, and everyone knows he trod on plenty of people to get there. Ginny watches the Apollo 14 EVA on television, just like the rest of America, marvelling at the colour footage broadcast direct from the lunar surface.

Yet for all the *realness* of the television pictures, in stark contrast to the blurred black-and-white of the Apollo 11 landing—and the picture quality for Apollo 14 is not that good, a bit blurry, the picture occasionally breaking up—but there's a seriousness to the way Al and Ed go about their activities on the lunar surface, and to Ginny it's like something is missing... the excitement, the wonder, the *fun*.

134

So she rises from the sofa, turns her back on the television, and goes into the yard. The sky is clear but it's only mid-morning and she can't see the Moon, not even a ghostly presentiment of it, the temperature is in the mid-fifties and the air is still. She hugs her torso and she shivers as she realises only a few months and Walden will be up there, a quarter of a million miles away. She thinks about the cost of the Apollo program, the deaths and broken marriages, and her own loneliness for much of that time. With Ramstein and Edwards, it has been a mostly lonely life since she left SDSU, just Walden and herself, her science fiction pen pals, the handful of wives she's become friends with, in USAF and NASA...

And via some chain of thought she cannot explain, she wonders if it was wrong to deny Walden, to deny herself, children. She was sensible about it, she prided herself on her good sense, and she was grateful their childlessness allowed her to live her own life... of sorts. But Walden has been away so much since he joined NASA, and even more so these last two years after being assigned to Apollo 15, and she wonders now if she made a mistake.

No, damn it. If she has dreams, they're of visiting other planets, not of diapers and pacifiers. She turns on her heel and re-enters the house. Apollo 14 is still on the television, but she ignores it. She stalks to the bedroom, takes the typewriter and paper from the closet, her folder of stories from her dressing table, and sets herself up at the dining table. She flicks through the stories she has written, and finds the one about the spacecraft in the decaying lunar orbit.

And to the sounds of Al Shepard and Ed Mitchell setting up experiments in the Fra Mauro Highlands on the Moon, she tries to inject some excitement, some wonder, some *fun* into her story, although truth be told there's not much fun in having to escape a spacecraft before it impacts the lunar surface and then floating around in lunar orbit for hours until rescue is possible...

HADLEY-APENNINE LANDING SITE

The Apollo 15 landing site is located at 26° 04' 54" North latitude by 3° 39' 30" East longitude at the foot of the Apennine mountain range. The Apennines rise up to more than 15,000 feet along the southeastern edge of the Mare Imbrium (Sea of Rains).

The Apennine escarpment--highest on the Moon--is higher above the flatlands than the east face of the Sierra Nevadas in California and the Himalayan front rising above the plains of Indian and Nepal. The landing site has been selected to allow astronauts Scott and Eckhardt to drive from the LM to the Apennine front during two of the EVAs.

A meandering canyon, Rima Hadley (Hadley Rille), approaches the Apennine front near the landing site and the combination of lurain provides an opportunity for the crew to explore and sample a mare basin, a mountain front and a lunar rille in a single mission.

Hadley Rille is a V-shaped gorge paralleling the Apennines along the eastern edge of Mare Imbrium. The rille meanders down from an elongated depression in the mountains and across the Palus Putredenis (Swamp of Decay), merging with a second rille about 62 miles (100 kilometers) to the north. Hadley rille averages about a kilometer and a half in width and about 1,300 feet (400 meters) in depth throughout most of its length.

Mount Hadley, Hadley Rille and the various Hadley craters in the region of the landing site are named for British scientist-mathematician John Hadley (1682-1744) who made improvements in reflector telescope design and invented the reflecting quadrant--an ancestor of the mariner's sextant.

Whatever Ginny did, it worked. Evelyn buys 'Pericynthion' for *Galaxy* within days of receiving it, and in her letter writes she really likes the idea of women astronauts, presented as if it were a perfectly normal and natural thing, and she especially admires Ginny's decision to mention no men at all in the story. Ginny knows her three year drought is finally over, so she rewrites the story about the astronaut who finds ancient alien ruins on Mars, but this time she gives her protagonist a family and that provides the motive to overcome disaster. Ginny retitles the story 'The Secret of Cydonia', a reference to one of Leigh's novels, and because Ginny likes the sound of the name "Cydonia".

And that one sells too—Kay takes it for *Astounding*, and she wants more like it. But Ginny now has bigger plans, a novella set on the Moon; but it's Apollo 15, Walden's flight, first, so on the second year anniversary of the first landing on the Moon, Ginny catches a commercial flight to Orlando, reading her July issue of *Galaxy*, which arrived only a couple of days before, and there's her name on the contents page, alongside Raccoona Sheldon and Joanna Russ and Joan Patricia Basch; but when the air hostess comes round, Ginny swaps the magazine for a copy of *Cosmopolitan*, although she's not looking at the fashion spreads she's thinking about *Galaxy* and she's thinking about Apollo 15.

The Saturn V slowly rises from Launch Pad 39A on its 8.5 million pounds of thrust, the roar of its engines crashing and breaking across the Florida swamps, a tidal wave of sound inundating the watchers on the stand, who have all risen to their feet. Fire pours from the F1 rocket engines, a small and dazzlingly bright sun on which the rocket is precariously balanced, and Ginny raises a hand to shade her eyes even though she is wearing sunglasses. She is over a mile away but the sheer physicality of the liftoff overwhelms her. The noise! The brightness! That slim pencil of black and white rising slowly up the sky on an infernal pillar. This is no science fiction spaceship launch, this is the real thing. There are very few examples she can recall from movies, Hollywood has yet to embrace science fiction, despite such 1920s classics as *Metropolis* and *Frau im*

Mond. It is a subject, they have discovered, best avoided. "Women's pictures" are one thing, but there is not a large enough audience with sufficient money to spend to justify making "sci fi" movies. Horror movies, yes, young men like them; and beach movies, too. But not science fiction.

This, however, the Saturn V, oh the flame and thunder!, spearing up into the sky, and now it's pitching over and seems to be travelling almost horizontal to the ground, heading for orbit, and thence to the Moon. Ginny's heart is in her mouth, she puts up a hand as if to prevent it escaping. She knows how perilous a mission this is, though the previous four Apollo flights have all gone pretty much as planned, at least up until the actual trip to the Moon...

She imagines Walden in his spacesuit sitting in the command module, that wide grey expanse of instrument panel above him shaking, she imagines him on the surface of the Moon, skipping across a sea of grey regolith. Godspeed, she tells him under her breath, though the religious sentiment means nothing to her. And she thinks about the novella she plans to start when she returns to Houston. She can almost see the first few lines:

```
Some days, when it feels like the end of the
world yet again, Vanessa Peterson, goes out
onto the surface and gazes up at what they
have lost.
     In the grey gunpowder dust, she stands in
the pose so familiar from televised missions.
She leans forward to counterbalance the
weight of the PLSS on her back; the A7LB's
inflated bladder pushes her arms out from her
sides. And she stares up at that grey-white
marble fixed mockingly above the horizon. She
listens to the whirr of the pumps, her own
```

breath an amniotic susurrus within the
confines of her helmet. The noises reassure
her--sound itself she finds comforting in
this magnificent desolation.

Ginny turns to Lurton, and she wishes Pam were here to
see this but it's been two years since the divorce; and Ginny
is surprised Lurton's face does not echo her own expression
of wonder, but then Ginny remembers she has a different
view of the space program to the other wives, and it's a
view she has never shared with them. So she turns back to
watch the Saturn V as it slowly fades from view, though the
roar of its launch seems to echo still across the inlets and
scrub, and Ginny is briefly amused by the Saturn V's phallic
symbolism, although that's been a staple of science fiction
since its beginnings—and what does that say about the
women who call themselves fans!—but this rocket, Wernher
von Braun's Saturn V, is to Ginny emphatically not one of
those symbolic images, because she's aware of the
engineering that has gone into it. When people see a LM,
they think of it as ugly but strangely functional in
appearance; but Ginny, she thinks about its incredibly thin
walls, all those switches and buttons, the guidance
computer and its programs, all the engineering it embodies.
And she thinks about standing inside the LM, a hand
gripping each hand controller, peering through the
triangular window before her at the surface of the Moon—
but the *real* lunar surface, not a simulated one.

She feels wetness on her cheek and, surprised, reaches
up to remove her sunglasses and dislodge a tear leaking
from one eye.

Primly stable, whispers Lurton.

An older woman, the wife of a senator, Ginny thinks,
Hart, something like that, she touches Ginny comfortingly
on the shoulder and says, He'll be fine, dear. You'll see.
You're married to a proper hero.

The comment prompts a wan smile. Walden, a hero. She guesses he is, the way he risks his life for science and engineering on a daily basis; but Ginny and Lurton, they're heroes too, because there's always the possibility of that knock on the door, the neighbour come round to keep them company until some grim-faced male colleague turns up. And there's keeping the home together, pretending they're as confident about the mission as the men, presenting a model marriage and family to NASA and the world. Because Ginny knows about the hardware, she knows that those first fifteen seconds, as the Saturn V rises to clear the gantry, those are the most dangerous—because if one of the five F1 rocket engines fails, there's still so much fuel aboard the other four wouldn't be able to lift the rocket's weight. Ginny knows this, and she's pretty sure the others on the stand don't.

Yet, despite everything she knows about the Saturn V and the Apollo command module and lunar module, despite everything Walden has explained to her, the guys at the Cape and back in Houston have explained to her, and she has read in the manuals and press kits, despite all this she knows Walden will come back home safely. She is convinced of that.

No, Ginny is not crying because she is worried she might never see her husband again. She is crying because she so badly wants to be in his place, to be crammed into that tiny command module heading for the Moon.

She is crying because she is watching her husband live *her* dream. She thinks of the years ahead, the nights she will spend sleeping beside, making love to, a man who has walked on the Moon. Her only way to cope is to take something she loves and refashion it so she can lay her impossible dream to rest within it. She will continue to rewrite the space program in science fiction as an entirely female enterprise because it is all she can do.

But no matter how audacious, it will never be a substitute—and she knows the pain of it will never fade.

Working name of US writer Virginia Grace Eckhardt
(1936 -), née Parker. She began publishing work of
genre interest with "Illgotten Gains" in Fantastic in June
1961. Parker is perhaps best known for the story "The
Spaceships Men Don't See" (February 1968 Galaxy), a
story based on the Fortean phenomenon the Philadelphia
Experiment and now seen as a direct bridge between so-
called housewife heroine sf, and feminist science fiction
(see Feminism). Although not especially well-regarded at
the time, the story was later re-appraised following
James Tiptree Jr's reference to it in "The Women Men
Don't See" (December 1973 F&SF). Parker was at her
most prolific from 1961 to 1965 but made only
intermittent magazine appearances in the years
following. Her last published science fiction, the novella
"Hard Vacuum" (September 1972 Analog), describes a
group of female astronauts trapped at a lunar base (see
Moon), and is notable for its technical detail; she
undoubtedly made use of the expertise of her then-
husband Walden J Eckhardt, Lunar Module Pilot for the
Apollo 15 mission to the Moon. After the lack of success
of "Hard Vacuum", Parker subsequently stopped
producing fiction and turned to writing nonfiction; a book
about the Mercury 13, *Lady Astronauts* (**1980**),
followed, and then *Aiming for the Stars* (**1986**), a
biography of Dr Sally Ride, the first American woman in
space. [JC/DRL]

Virginia Grace Eckhardt

born San Diego, California: 4 December 1936

Extract from the Encyclopedia of Science Fiction, www.sf-encyclopedia.com

APPENDICES

NOTES

- Galaxy table of contents adapted from Galaxy Magazine, February 1968, Vol 26 No. 3
- neither Virginia Leith, Grace Kelly nor Suzy Parker starred in more than a dozen feature films each. Some are definitely worth seeing. Virginia Leith: VIOLENT SATURDAY (1955), ON THE THRESHOLD OF SPACE (1956), A KISS BEFORE DYING (1956), TOWARD THE UNKNOWN (1956), THE BRAIN THAT WOULDN'T DIE (1962). Grace Kelly: HIGH NOON (1952), MOGAMBO (1953), DIAL M FOR MURDER (1954), REAR WINDOW (1954), THE BRIDGES AT TOKO-RI (1954), THE COUNTRY GIRL (1954), GREEN FIRE (1954), TO CATCH A THIEF (1955), THE SWAN (1956), HIGH SOCIETY (1956). Suzy Parker: KISS THEM FOR ME (1957), TEN NORTH FREDERICK (1958), THE BEST OF EVERYTHING (1959), A CIRCLE OF DECEPTION (1960), THE INTERNS (1962), FLIGHT FROM ASHIYA (1964).
- NASA Group 6 news release adapted from NASA news release 66-022: www.nasa.gov/centers/johnson/news/releases/1966_1968/
- artwork for 'The Spaceships Men Don't See' by Ian Sales
- LM Crew Compartment Familiarization Phase I A taken from LUNAR MODULE ORIENTATION GUIDE & COMPARTMENT FAMILIARIZATION, Robert Godwin (20019, Apogee Books, 978-1-926592-11-4)
- Galaxy LOC inspired by real letters in Galaxy Magazine, February 1975, Vol. 36, No. 2
- the Judith Merril story is, of course, 'The Lady Was a Tramp', although the real version has the genders reversed as described here
- Lunar Module (LM) insert taken from Apollo 15 press kit: http://history.nasa.gov/alsj/a15/A15_PressKit.pdf
- Wal Eckhardt Wikipedia entry adapted from the Wikipedia entry on James B Irwin, and used under Creative Commons licence
- table of A7L materials taken from Smithsonian National Air and Space Museum web site: http://airandspace.si.edu/explore-and-learn/multimedia/detail.cfm?id=5219

- Apollo 11 EVA transcript excerpt taken from Apollo 11 Lunar Surface Journal
- Apollo 15 Launch NASA news release adapted from Apollo 15 press kit: http://history.nasa.gov/alsj/a15/A15_PressKit.pdf
- Hadley-Apennine Landing Site excerpt take from Apollo 15 press kit: http://history.nasa.gov/alsj/a15/A15_PressKit.pdf
- SF Encyclopedia entry on VG Parker: layout used by kind permission, and editorial assistance, of the Encyclopedia of Science Fiction, www.sf-encyclopedia.com

YOU HAVE BEEN READING ABOUT...
writers and editors

Joan Patricia Basch (published 1966 to 1967)

Faye Beslow (published 1952 to 1953)

Doris Pitkin Buck (published 1952 to 1975)

Jane Beauclerk (AKA MJ Engh, published 1964 to 1995)

Leigh Brackett (published 1940 to 1976)

Betsy Curtis (published 1950 to 1973)

Miriam Allen deFord (published 1946 to 1974)

Gertrude Friedberg (published 1958 to 1972)

Alice Eleanor Jones (published 1955)

Cele Goldsmith (editor, 1957 to 1965)

Clare Winger Harris (published 1926 to 1930)

Hazel Heald (published 1932 to 1935)

Zenna Henderson (published 1951 to 1982)

Ursula K Le Guin (published 1961 to present)

June Lurie (published 1946 to 1953)

Linda Marlowe (published 1967)

Anne McCaffrey (published 1953 to 2011)

Judith Merril (published 1948 to 1985)

CL 'Catherine' Moore (published 1930 to 1958)

Andre 'Alice' Norton (published 1939 to 2004)

Evelyn Paige (editor, 1951 to 1956)

Doris Piserchia (published 1966 to 1983)

Kit Reed (published 1958 to present)

Joanna Russ (published 1959 to 1996)

Josephine Saxton (published 1965 to 1992)

Monica Sterba (AKA Frances Oliver, published 1964 to 2010)

Francis Stevens (AKA Gertrude Burrows Bennett, published 1904 to 1923)

Leslie F Stone (published 1929 to 1940)

Kay Tarrant (editor, 1942 to 1972)

James Tiptree Jr (AKA Alice B 'Ali' Sheldon, Raccoona Sheldon, published 1968 to 1987)

Susan Trott (published 1967)
Sydney J Van Scyoc (published 1962 to 2005)
Kate Wilhelm (published 1956 to 2012)

astronaut wives club

Joan Aldrin (Fourteen)
Valerie Anders (Fourteen)
Janet Armstrong (New Nine)
Jeannie Bassett (Fourteen)
Sue Bean (Fourteen)
Susan Borman (New Nine)
Joan Brand (Original Nineteen)
Nancy Bull (Original Nineteen)
Rene Carpenter (Original Seven)
JoAnn Carr (Original Nineteen)
Barbara Cernan (Fourteen)
Martha Chaffee (Fourteen)
Pat Collins (Fourteen)
Jane Conrad (New Nine)
Trudy Cooper (Original Seven)
Loella Cunningham (Fourteen)
Dotty Duke (Original Nineteen)
Harriet Eisele (Fourteen)
Mary Engle (Original Nineteen)
Jan Evans (Original Nineteen)
Faith Freeman (Fourteen)
Ada Givens (Original Nineteen)
Barbara Gordon (Fourteen)
Betty Grissom (Original Seven)
Mary Haise (Original Nineteen)
Kathleen Lind (Original Nineteen)
Grati Lousma (Original Nineteen)
Marilyn Lovell (New Nine)
Liz Mattingly (Original Nineteen)
Bernice McCandless (Original Nineteen)

Pat McDivitt (New Nine)
Louise Mitchell (Original Nineteen)
Wanita Pogue (Original Nineteen)
Joan Roosa (Original Nineteen)
Jo Schirra (Original Seven)
Clare Schweikart (Fourteen)
Lurton Scott (Fourteen)
Marilyn See (New Nine)
Louise Shepard (Original Seven)
Marge Slayton (Original Seven)
Faye Stafford (New Nine)
Susan Weitz (Original Nineteen)
Pat White (New Nine)
Beth Williams (Fourteen)
Pam Worden (Original Nineteen)
Barbara Young (New Nine)
...and Mary Irwin (Original Nineteen)

astronauts

Buzz Aldrin, USAF (Gemini 12, Apollo 11 LMP)
Bill Anders, USAF (Apollo 8 LMP)
Neil Armstrong, civ (Gemini 8, Apollo 11 commander)
Charlie Bassett, USAF (died during training)
Al Bean, USN (Apollo 12 LMP)
Frank Borman, USAF (Gemini 7, Apollo 8 commander)
Scott Carpenter, USN (Aurora 7)
Gene Cernan, USN (Gemini 9A, Apollo 10 LMP, Apollo 17
    commander)
Roger Chaffee, USN (died Apollo 1 fire)
Pete Conrad, USN (Gemini 5, Gemini 11, Apollo 12 commander)
Michael Collins, USAF (Gemini 10, Apollo 11 CMP)
Gordo Cooper, USAF (Faith 7, Gemini 5)
Walter Cunningham, USMC (Apollo 7 LMP)
Charlie Duke, USAF (Apollo 16 LMP)
Donn Eisele, USAF (Apollo 7 CMP)

Joe Engle, USAF (did not fly in Apollo program)

Ron Evans, USN (Apollo 17 CMP)

Teddy Freeman, USAF (died during training)

Dick Gordon, USN (Gemini 11, Apollo 12 CMP)

Gus Grissom, USAF (Liberty Bell 7, Gemini 3, died Apollo 1 fire)

Fred Haise, civ (Apollo 13 LMP)

Jim Lovell, USN (Gemini 7, Gemini 12, Apollo 8 CMP, Apollo 13 commander)

Ken Mattingly, USN (Apollo 16 CMP)

Ed Mitchell, USN (Apollo 14 LMP)

Jim McDivitt, USAF (Gemini 4, Apollo 9 commander)

Stu Roosa, USAF (Apollo 14 CMP)

Elliot See, civ (died during training)

Wally Schirra, USN (Sigma 7, Gemini 6A, Apollo 7 commander)

Rusty Schweickart, USAF (Apollo 9 LMP)

Dave Scott, USAF (Gemini 8, Apollo 9 CMP, Apollo 15 commander)

Alan Shepard, USN (Freedom 7, Apollo 14 commander)

Deke Slayton, USAF (ASTP docking module pilot)

Tom Stafford, USAF (Gemini 6A, Gemini 9A, Apollo 10 commander)

Jack Swigert, civ (Apollo 13 CMP)

Ed White, USAF (Gemini 4, died Apollo 1 fire)

Clifton Williams, USMC (died during training)

Al Worden, USAF (Apollo 15 CMP)

John Young, USN (Gemini 3, Gemini 10, Apollo 10 CMP, Apollo 16 commander)

... and Jim Irwin, USAF (Apollo 15 LMP)

others

Dee O'Hara, chief nurse to the astronauts

Joe Schmitt, suit technician

Cecilia Payne-Gaposchkin, British-American astronomer

Janey Hart, aviator and member of the Mercury 13

FURTHER READING

_Arnason, Eleanor: 'The Warlord of Saturn's Moons'
   (1974, NEW WORLDS 7, ed. Hilary Bailey & Charles Platt)
_Dorman, Sonya: 'When I Was Miss Dow'
   (1966, GALAXY MAGAZINE, Jun 1966)
_Emshwiller, Carol: 'Idol's Eye'
   (1958, FUTURE SCIENCE FICTION #35, Feb 1958)
_Fowler, Karen Joy: 'What I Didn't See'
   (2002, SCI FICTION, Jul 2002)
_Jones, Alice Eleanor: 'Created He Them'
   (1955, THE MAGAZINE OF FANTASY & SCIENCE FICTION, Jun 1955)
_Merril, Judith: 'That Only A Mother'
   (1948, ASTOUNDING SCIENCE FICTION, Jun 1948)
___: 'Daughters of Earth'
   (1952, THE PETRIFIED PLANET, No ISBN)
_Reed, Kit: 'Songs of War'
   (1974, NOVA 4, ed. Harry Harrison)
_Russ, Joanna: 'When It Changed'
   (1972, AGAIN, DANGEROUS VISIONS, ed. Harlan Ellison)
___: 'An Old-Fashioned Girl'
   (1974, FINAL STAGE, ed. Edward L Ferman & Barry N Malzberg)
_Saxton, Josephine: 'The Triumphant Head'
   (1970, ALCHEMY AND ACADEME, ed. Anne McCaffrey)
___: 'Dormant Soul'
   (1969, THE MAGAZINE OF FANTASY & SCIENCE FICTION, Feb 1969)
_Tiptree Jr, James: 'The Women Men Don't See'
   (1973, THE MAGAZINE OF FANTASY & SCIENCE FICTION, Dec 1973)
_Tuttle, Lisa: 'Wives'
   (1979, THE MAGAZINE OF FANTASY & SCIENCE FICTION, Dec 1979)
_Wilhelm, Kate: 'The Funeral'
   (1972, AGAIN, DANGEROUS VISIONS, ed. Harlan Ellison)
_Zoline, Pamela: 'The Heat Death of the Universe'
   (1967, NEW WORLDS SPECULATIVE FICTION, Jul 1967)

Many of these stories have been subsequently collected and are
available in a variety of venues. Check www.isfdb.org for details.

BIBLIOGRAPHY

_Armstrong, Neil, Michael Collins & Edwin E Aldrin Jr: FIRST ON THE
    MOON (1970, Little, Brown, No ISBN)
_Bostick, Michael, Brian Grazer & Ron Howard: FROM THE EARTH TO THE
    MOON (1998, Clavius Base, Go Flight Inc, Imagine Entertainment)
_Bowman, Martin W: STRATOFORTRESS, THE STORY OF THE B-52
    (2005, Pen & Sword, 1-84415-234-0)
_Brookes, Courtney G, James M Grimwood & Loyd S Swenson Jr:
    CHARIOTS FOR APOLLO: A HISTORY OF MANNED LUNAR SPACECRAFT
    (1979, NASA, No ISBN)
_Caidin, Martin: THE CAPE
    (1971, Doubleday, No ISBN)
_Davin, Eric Leif: PARTNERS IN WONDER
    (2006, Lexington Books, 978-0-7391-1267-0)
_de Monchaux, Nicholas: SPACESUIT - FASHIONING APOLLO
    (2011, The MIT Press, 978-0-262-01520-2)
_Dethloff, Henry C: SUDDENLY, TOMORROW CAME... A HISTORY OF THE
    JOHNSON SPACE CENTER (1993, NASA, No ISBN)
_Donner, Richard: X-15
    (1961, Essex Productions)
_Duke Charlie & Dotty: MOONWALKER
    (1990, Oliver Nelson, 0-8407-9106-2)
_Friedan, Betty: THE FEMININE MYSTIQUE
    (1963, Penguin, 0-14-002261-9)
_Godwin, Robert: APOLLO 11: THE NASA MISSION REPORTS VOLUME 1
    (1999, Apogee Books, 1-896522-53-X)
_Godwin, Robert: APOLLO 12: THE NASA MISSION REPORTS
    (1999, Apogee Books, 1-896522-54-8)
_Gurney, Gene: AMERICANS INTO ORBIT
    (1962, Landmark Books, No ISBN)
_Irwin, James B: TO RULE THE NIGHT
    (1973, AJ Holman Company, 0-87981-024-6)
_Irwin, Mary: THE MOON IS NOT ENOUGH
    (1978, Pickering & Inglis, 0-7028-0446-9)
_Kaufman, Philip: THE RIGHT STUFF
    (1983, The Ladd Company)
_Koppel, Lily: THE ASTRONAUT WIVES CLUB

(2013, Headline, 978-0-7553-6259-2)
_Kraft, Chris: FLIGHT: MY LIFE IN MISSION CONTROL
    (2001, Dutton, 0-525-94571-7)
_Kranz, Gene: FAILURE IS NOT AN OPTION
    (2000, Simon & Schuster, 0-7432-0079-9)
_LeRoy, Mervyn: TOWARD THE UNKNOWN
    (1956, Toluca Productions)
_Larbalestier, Justine: THE BATTLE OF THE SEXES IN SCIENCE FICTION
    (2002, Wesleyan University Press, 0-8195-6527-X)
_Larbalestier, Justine, ed.: DAUGHTERS OF EARTH
    (2006, Wesleyan University Press, 978-0-8195-6676-8)
_Mallick, Donald L: THE SMELL OF KEROSENE: A TEST PILOT'S ODYSSEY
    (2003, NASA, No ISBN)
_Merril, Judith & Emily Pohl-Weary: BETTER TO HAVE LOVED
    (2002, Between The Lines, 1-896357-57-1)
_Michener, James A: SPACE
    (1982, Random House, 0-394-50555-7)
_Moseley, Willie G: SMOKE JUMPER, MOON PILOT
    (2011, Acclaim Press, 978-1-935001-76-8)
_Phillips, Julie: JAMES TIPTREE, JR: THE DOUBLE LIFE OF
    ALICE B SHELDON (2006, Picador, 978-0-312-42694-1)
_Saxton, Josephine: THE POWER OF TIME
    (1985, Chatto & Windus, 0-7011-2955-7)
_Scott, David & Alexei Leonov: TWO SIDES OF THE MOON
    (2004, Simon & Schuster, 0-7342-3162-7)
_Sirk, Douglas: ALL THAT HEAVEN ALLOWS
    (1955, Universal International Pictures)
_Stafford, Tom: WE HAVE CAPTURE
    (2002, Smithsonia Institute Press, 1-58834-070-8)
_Thoreau, Henry David: WALDEN; OR A LIFE IN THE WOODS
    (1854, Gutenberg Project, No ISBN)
_Webb, Robert D: ON THE THRESHOLD OF SPACE
    (1956, Twentieth Century Fox)
_Worden, Al, with Francis French: FALLING TO EARTH
    (2011, Smithsonian Books, 978-1-58834-309-3)
_Yaszek, Lisa: GALACTIC SUBURBIA
    (2008, The Ohio State University Press, 978-0-8142-5164-5)

ONLINE SOURCES

Apollo Flight Journal
    history.nasa.gov/afj/
Apollo Operations Handbook
    history.nasa.gov/afj/aohindex.htm
Astronaut Wives Club Tumblr
    astronautwivesclub.tumblr.com
Beyond Apollo
    www.wired.com/category/science-blogs/beyondapollo/
collectSPACE
    www.collectspace.com
Encyclopedia Astronautica
    www.astronautix.com/
The Internet Science Fiction Database, ISFDB
    www.isfdb.org
The Project Apollo Image Gallery
    www.apolloarchive.com/apollo_gallery.html
Science Fiction Encyclopedia
    www.sf-encyclopedia.com
Wikipedia
    en.wikipedia.org

ABOUT THE AUTHOR

Ian Sales wanted to be an astronaut when he grew up, but sadly wasn't born in the USA or USSR. So he writes about them instead. He also owns a large number of books on the subject. Ian has had fiction published in a number of science fiction and literary magazines and original. In 2012, he edited the anthology *Rocket Science* for Mutation Press. In 2013, he won the BSFA Award for *Adrift on the Sea of Rains* and was nominated for the Sidewise Award for the same work. In 2015, the first two books of a space opera trilogy, *A Prospect of War* and *A Conflict of Orders*, will be published by Tickety Boo Press. Ian reviews books for *Interzone*, and is represented by the John Jarrold Literary Agency. You can find him online at www.iansales.com and on Twitter as @ian_sales.

ACKNOWLEDGEMENTS

A great many thanks to beta readers—Craig Andrews, Eric Brown, Cliff Burns, Dave Hutchinson, Michael Martineck, Jonathan McCalmont, Glen Mehn, Maureen Kincaid Speller and Deborah Walker; Jim Steel for editorial duties; Kay Sales for cover art; and my agent, John Jarrold. This one had a difficult gestation, hence the long period between *Then Will The Great Ocean Wash Deep Above* and its appearance And the fact it's novel-length. I hope the wait— and the wordcount—was worth it.

ALSO BY WHIPPLESHIELD BOOKS

The Apollo Quartet, Ian Sales

1 Adrift on the Sea of Rains (2012)
- paperback (2nd edn)   £4.99 / $7.50 / €6.00
- ebook: PDF, EPUB, MOBI   £2.99 / $3.99 / €2.99

2 The Eye With Which The Universe Beholds Itself (2012)
- paperback (2nd edn)   £4.99 / $7.50 / €6.00
- signed numbered hardback   £6.99 / $12.00 / €8.50
- ebook: PDF, EPUB, MOBI   £2.99 / $3.99 / €2.99

3 Then Will The Great Ocean Wash Deep Above (2013)
- paperback (2nd edn)   £4.99 / $7.50 / €6.00
- signed numbered hardback   £6.99 / $10.00 / €8.50
- ebook: PDF, EPUB, MOBI   £2.99 / $3.99 / €2.99

4 All That Outer Space Allows (2015)
- paperback   £7.99 / $9.50 / €9.00
- signed numbered hardback   £9.99 / $13.00 / €11.50
- ebook: PDF, EPUB, MOBI   £2.99 / $3.99 / €2.99

Printed in Great Britain
by Amazon.co.uk, Ltd.,
Marston Gate.